# I.N.NARDS

# INNARDS

*stories*

# Magogodi oaMphela Makhene

**W. W. NORTON & COMPANY**
*Celebrating a Century of Independent Publishing*

"Indians Can't Fly" first published by *The Drift* © 2023 by Magogodi oaMphela Makhene, "Dr. Basters" first published by *American Short Fiction* © 2022 by Magogodi oaMphela Makhene, "The Caretaker" first published by *Ploughshares* © 2016 by Magogodi oaMphela Makhene, "The Virus" first published by *Harvard Review* © 2016 by Magogodi oaMphela Makhene, "Jesus Owes Me Money" first published by *Guernica* magazine © 2013 by Magogodi oaMphela Makhene are reprinted by permission of the author and Aragi Inc. "Innards" first published by *Granta* © 2019 by Magogodi oaMphela Makhene is reprinted by permission of the author.

For information about permission to reproduce selections from this book, write to Permissions, W. W. Norton & Company, Inc., 500 Fifth Avenue, New York, NY 10110

For information about special discounts for bulk purchases, please contact W. W. Norton Special Sales at specialsales@wwnorton.com or 800-233-4830

Manufacturing by Lakeside Book Company
Book design by Beth Steidle
Production manager: Anna Oler

ISBN 978-1-324-05100-8

W. W. Norton & Company, Inc.
500 Fifth Avenue, New York, N.Y. 10110
www.wwnorton.com

W. W. Norton & Company Ltd.
15 Carlisle Street, London W1D 3BS

3 4 5 6 7 8 9 0

*For our Gods, my ever-living ancestors:*

*bagaMphela le baNkadimeng. Bare kwena ga e tsene metseng!*
*bagaMakhene le baSepeng. Kgabo tse dinhle!*
*For my grandparents especially—Johanna Togoloane Mahlako*
*and Edward Kwetjane Mphela.*

*And for Mommy, Dimakatso Maks Mmadiphisho Mphela*
*Makhene—this praise song is for you!*

# *Contents*

# I.N.NARDS

# *Bua*

*Everyone claims ancestral royalty. Even slaves. No one* imagines their beginning damned or marred by mediocrity. No. The likely telling is of glory. Of kings and paramount chiefs prostrating themselves like bush rabbits fearing our forefathers— those fearsome foxes. Of queen mothers throwing their firstborn daughters into our bloodstream like eager spawn sifting salt water for sperm.

*Our star was born long-tailed*, the old man liked to say. *We were kingmakers and twin sires. Even our cows came in pairs. We made rain fall in Great Zimbabwe.*

No one asks him, How, then, did the Boers and the British happen? How did such a strong and certain seed turn slave on its own ancestral land?

So much of who we are is fiction. The old man's wife used to tell him that. And that only a woman could be God. Only Woman—who takes heat, sweat and sin and turns it into flesh; into sacred being.

Carrying life teaches you that, she'd say.

Maybe that's why history forgets our grandmothers. They are written in the womb.

# 7678B
# Old Potchefstroom Road

*They came riding cattle lorries. Their whole world traveling* with them, herded onto truck flatbacks. Thick woolen blankets folded into warm wishes. Matching chairs and lorry-scratched dining tables bought piecemeal on layaway. And head-scarved Granny, wrapped at the waist in a brown plaid blanket that doubled as cot when the baby fussed.

Out, those cattle wagons drove. Out. Past the city, Park Station behind them and old Ferreirasdorp decaying with the sunset. Out, meandering with Commissioner Street beyond an empty yellow wasteland dumped by Crown Mines. Out and into a barren veld bordered on either side by municipal sewerage farms.

They came like that, curious about this place. Curiouser still— entire families and their lives packed into the same space where a lamb probably hoof-kneaded sheep shit on its way to the slaughterhouse yesterday. The lorry beds were all metal and wooden plank, with mesh cage roofs like a chicken coop. Swine haulers, those lorries, now overloaded with babies, steamer trunks and loose cupboard drawers. Everything unhinged.

I wasn't sure which family was mine. And by the standing

around and waiting, pointing at numbers, eyes searching, these natives themselves seemed uncertain which of us was whose.

A short man with an orange mustache and a squat face took control, clipboard in hand, a neat row of pencils peeking from pocket. "Yebo Baas," the men answered him, showing their dompass. The Baas then gave each man a key with his number. Some slipped a few shillings into his hand for another number promising an indoor toilet. Then they packed off for this house. A thin mattress balancing on the wife's head. A heavy washtub carried one-one on either side by the children.

—7678B? Clipboard Baas called my name. A man in a dark suit walked toward me, his wife behind—her white heels stepping into his imprints, so that their soles cleaved to one another in the dust. The children's weren't far behind. Stop, Granny shouted, *Stop! Stop that running!* But the mother was running, catching her husband's shadow and moving past him, toward me. He watched her; let her. So that a woman first entered my threshold.

Her heels were soiled by now, the color of rust, but she didn't notice, running into my rooms, thrusting windows to the world, standing with her arms the width of my walls. As if embracing my full girth, everything inside me. As if to say, Yes. This will do.

Only with her children also running in and out of the rooms— rooms so small they could be folded up and stuffed into the lorry-fastened wardrobe—only then did the dirt floor disappoint her. Little feet kicked up dust and stone. The wife looked around, shushing the children, but her gaze met her husband's and the steady smile growing on Granny's face. We'll have to plaster, she said. And . . . paint.

≫≫≍≪≪

Men arrived. In long trousers that sat low, far low, below bare chests and taupe sweat. Ethel—I know her name now—Ethel hummed as she cooked, knifing tenderly through gummy seeds, fingering small tastes to her tongue. The smell of fried onion skin sizzling in sunflower oil and ripe tomatoes filled me, as if I were lungs.

She brought a tray out to the men. The tray held a small washbasin with soapy water and a clean cloth. Next to this was a large dish offering last night's leftovers fattened with fresh tomato gravy. Ethel bent to pass the cloth and washbasin around, putting the food on the ground. Bodies close, she smelled how the sun made itself rancid on the men's skin. She wound her neck—slowly, absently. When she took her lunch inside with Granny, her fingers caressed her nape just as absently, the same space between neck and spine that Tom's hands and tongue had chiseled smooth late last night.

—It's quite tasty, Granny said.

—Yes, Ethel smiled, e monate.

Tom—Ethel's husband—was the sole sound I heard whispering to the night. It was quiet. Ethel was quiet, nervous their hunger would stir the children. She forced her pleasure into the pillow. A pleasure as silent as muffled pain.

—Have you heard the one about the Boer and his missus? Tom asked.

—No, she shook her head, gently, as if a full head shake would wake the baby beside them and the children on the now plastered floor.

—The missus, said Tom.

—Asks her Baas . . .

Tom stopped. Chuckling.

—That's how krom daai man is, he says, still laughing.

—He orders his wife call him Baas!

Ethel smiled, wry. I could see her bare teeth flash at the asbestos roof that is my own mouth.

—Anyways, Tom goes on, the missus asks her Baas: *But where were you, just now getting in, so vroeg in the morning? Where did you spend the night?* The Boer scratches his head a bit and thinks quick on his feet:

—*Ag, man, vrou!* the skelm begins. *Woman! I was at that friend of you's. Susanna.*

Go on, the wife's face seems to say.

—*Well. Her husband took a turn. For the worse. And just like that . . . Poop!* He snaps a finger. *The hairy bliksem died. He's dead!* The Boeremeisie sniffles. *You know how you women are.* Seeing this, the Baas is bloody chuffed with himself, swelling at his stupid cleverness. He doesn't even notice his missus scratching about till she's fully dressed, fetching her gloves and looking for a scarf to cover her head.

—*Vrou?* he asks. *Waarheen nou?*

—*To Susanna's,* the missus replies. *She'll need to borrow you another night and maybe some other things also.*

—*Nee man!* says the Boer, quick-quick on his feet, again scratching that head.

—*They ring while you dressing. Turns out that old fat bastard isn't dead after all. He rose. Up! Just now-now. Like Jesus! He rose up from the dead!*

Ethel put a finger to Tom's lips, stifling their giggles. She peered over his body at the young ones, sleeping below the mattress. Little chests rose and fell with the deep breath of children's dreams.

More families arrived, taking up the empty numbers all around me, until the neighborhood pulsed with fat gossip at communal taps, with hammering nails shouting response to workmen songs. Radios belted out news from faraway places where news happens—places so scary the fear seeped through the speakers and settled beneath my trenched roots. Stray chickens wandered in. Flocks of ashy children pecked about the street in gray packs that smeared their idleness and wonder everywhere people sprouted. Life grew without record or resolve. Daily routine—sewerage bucket dumps early mornings and coal deliveries before sunset—made rhythm out of time.

E thel walked into the kitchen, tired, fed coal to the furnace and placed a large round-bottomed kettle on the boil. Her daughters, older now with small seeds of womanhood, clung to sleep under the table. She sang, softly, a silly song about a girl who slept past sunrise, her crops shriveling into snakes. The girls woke. Ethel poured a cup of black tea and carried a large tin tub, filled with Tom's bath, into their room.

Tom's suit jacket, pants and tie lay spread across the bed like a Kliptown jumble sale. His shirt hung from the door handle, a soft yellow stain warming its armpits. After washing, he reached first for a sleeveless undershirt, then his shirt. Ethel stood behind him, folding his work uniform—Tom never left or returned in anything but a suit, red-feathered fedora in hand. He unraveled his tie's knot for a fresh start: right end over left, mimicking the shape of a cross. He fussed, looking into the mirror, then at his wife's double.

—You look like someone getting late for work, Ethel said, naughty mischief overtaking her smile.

—But my shoes don't even shine yet, Tom pointed.

—Okay, okay, Mr. Very Important, High-Class, Top-Label Shoes.
You keep powdering your nose. You keep preening and primp-
ing and you'll really be late this time.

Quickly, in a single fluid motion, Tom spat spittle on the
shoes, rubbed hard with his polishing cloth and was out the door.

—Ehn!? Ethel called out, laughing.

—Mr. High-Class Shoes! She charged after him. What about
your uniform?

Tom walked out, barefoot and skinny-chested, soon worrying
earthworms between his spindly fingers, smelling the soil and
clamping its slight sweat. It was the weekend. He bent low to
the ground, digging beds for black arum lilies with a retooled
serving spoon, imagining the arums' elegant swan necks reaching one day beyond his knee. He came next to a frail jacaranda
sapling, carrying water to it on his head, like a woman. His
plants took root. They didn't believe, as authorities do, this land
too sterile—a suitable plot to blackspot with natives. Maybe it
was the sewerage fattening the soil. Engorging this parcel of
uncharted, unwanted earth.

Lording over Tom's Eden, as if greening the grass, was a red-
hatted gnome with a seriousness to his mischief—a voluminous
beard and furrowed brow, a plump but upright body and unseen,
hiding hands, held behind his back. I wasn't bothered by this
midget little he-man. Grass leaves must've seemed a thick forest
to his eyes, the distant hydrangeas an unreachable land. *I* could
see beyond the hydrangea hedge, to the invisible fence within its
branches. I could see beyond that even, to where the garden met
an unpaved road. Old Potchefstroom Road. Named for a sleepy
little dorp where Brits held Boers in concentration camps, before
the Boers built a giant concentration camp out of the whole
country.

Weekends also brought visitors. A brother or third cousin carrying urgent news from home.

—Buti, they called Tom.

—Your little uncle's son is marrying. The bride's father wants thirty bulls.

—Tjo! Tjo! Tjo! Someone would cluck their tongue, or whistle cleanly, or burst into spastic laughter.

Sometimes Tom had already heard about the trouble—about another relative stripped of his farmland by Verwoerd and the white man's law.

—Two hundred fifty rands? he'd ask, stacking the bills on the table. At least that'll get him some blankets. An unforgivable winter is coming, Tom would sigh.

Guests were received in the front room. At the proud dining table scratched by the cattle lorry on the drive out. Tom sat opposite his visitors—there wasn't enough room to squeeze a chair at the head. Ethel served tea on a tray, her sugar bowl matching the rose-blooming cups. The milk jug, also part of her set, had a jagged chip on the lip—like a pretty girl with knocked-out sawteeth. Visitors stayed for at least one meal. This was understood as soon as an unexpected but booming knock filled the house. Ko-ko-ko! the knuckles rapped, despite my front door standing wide ajar. If it was Sunday, the children cursed under silent breath, knowing a minor chicken piece would be split six ways between them, the coveted drumstick now firmly out of the question. Their next best hope was an empty bag. If the relative's sack was light, it held no overnight plans.

This was how Ethel's youngest brother, King, arrived. From Transkei. He showed up on a Sunday morning. Ncgo-ncgo-ncgo? His knock was light, uncertain. Come in! Ethel shouted, throwing her arms around him on seeing who it was. The girls—helping with chores, the boys playing outside—looked on, shy-like. He took off his hat and a tatty, threadbare jacket. He shook each girl's hand and asked their names in deep, rhythmic Xhosa. Kingsley carried not a single bag. He stayed a whole month.

Late nights, King hid outside. He'd climb into the big metallic coal bin. Sometimes it was full but he'd force his way in, parting the rock with his body. The police never checked the coal lockbox, hard to say why. And after each dompass raid, he'd emerge from the shiny bin sweaty and soot-black.

—Sister, he'd sulk, this is how you live?

But Ethel would only poke fun, mocking his Cape Colored–like blackface, sommer another Boesman cruising the Coon Carnival.

—So, King. You'd rather turn Colored than go in a mine shaft and sing *Môre! Baas*? Ethel would ask, laughing, trying to pump air back in the room by going straight for the jugular vein: Kingsley still hadn't found work. Which meant he had no white man to sign his papers. Which made Kingsley the thing they stamp in a dompass before deportation: "Prohibited Alien." But instead of Ethel's words stinging, Kingsley would strum an invisible guitar in response to the jabbing, everyone laughing. He'd bare his teeth through his coal-colored blackface, mimicking Coloreds mimicking black savages at their New Year's Eve minstrel show. The children would join in also, singing and blowing make-believe horns, clapping whatever they could find into tambourines.

Less than a month later, Kingsley gave Ethel another reason to play make-believe, this time with the old woman Makhadze. It was after Tom answered an unmistakable *Bang-Bang-Bang!* late one night. Someone tipped them off, Ethel later told Tom. The police had barely considered Tom's papers, swatting off his identity book like a clumsy flea.

—We hear you have a fat rat squatting around here, the black policeman boomed.

—Is that right? another asked Tom, making a show of tapping his baton.

What happened next is the two policemen walked Tom outside, toward the back of the yard, behind the toilet. Made him unlatch the box. Shined a blackout beam onto the peat rock. The coal lit up under torchlight, glistening, like something strangely beautiful. Like burning candlewick—so intently black. Or pools of oil resistant to rain.

*Somebody told them*, Ethel repeated in whispers. They'd blown out all the candles and crept into bed. The girls in the kitchen. Granny on the sofa and the boys under the scratched dining table. Everyone wide awake, pretending faraway sleep.

—You have to do something, Ethel begged Tom.

—Something like what? Tom's tone was sharp.

—Isn't it enough he wasn't in the box? They didn't catch him, Ethel. What else do you want me to do? Shit out a fresh dompass?

—Tom, please! Ethel pleaded. We don't even know where he's sleeping.

—He's a man, Ethel.

—A Missing Man!

Ethel never shouted, never raised her voice over Tom's. Tom sighed. Seeming to shrink from the effort.

—Every man passes through this, Ethy. You think we want to part our arse for the Baas and sleep in his jail cells?

It was harsh, what Tom was saying. But he said it soft and even, like a loaf of industrial-grade butter.

—King is a man, Ethel. He'll survive.


Makhadze lived in the dreamworld. She was known to fetch stubborn babies and their mischievous spirits who refused to wake from their ancestors' dreams and into birth. Whenever Ethel's moonbelly burst under secret tide, Makhadze was long in the room, preparing with Granny. Even Granny knew better than to argue with Makhadze. She'd ably delivered the twins after they came feet first. And she was rumored to have unsettled spirits sheltering beneath her bed. Makhadze disquieted me. She listened too intently, parsing out what others called house sounds. I held my breath, knowing Ethel trusted her. Needed her.

—She was an old woman, Ethel told Makhadze, describing a dream.

—Very old. Her skin pooled around her joints, like she could step out of herself if she wanted. A dark woman. Black. Black. Black. She kept smiling at me in the dream, but her eyes didn't light. Only her eyebags moved. When she smiled, her eyebags made me think she was a man. We slept on the floor—me and this old woman—back to back. Me facing the wall. I started nodding off but then I felt cold hands. Cold strong hands pressing my backside. Not shy. Firm. One-one, holding each cheek. I turned around to ask this gogo, *What's happening?* But her whole face was suddenly those heavy eyebags, twitching. And a beard grew fast and thick, covering her face. I started feeling very sick, Mme Makhadze. And when I woke, the vomit was also thick. Like rotten oats.

—Your dream is not good, Makhadze sniffed.

She carried a small container of snuff inside her skirt pockets.

—Chinaman is going to draw a penis or a dead woman today. Number thirty-six and Number twelve. If he draws the dead woman, your brother will live. But if it's a penis . . .

After Makhadze left, Granny cursed the wrinkly Venda matron a savage heathen.

—Sies! Granny said, I wouldn't wash my panties in water from that Makhadze's house.

—Phooh! Granny spat.

But Ethel wasn't listening.

The m'China who ran fahfee always appeared with the sunset. He was a stumpy man with a perfectly round face and upstanding imp ears. He spoke enough Zulu to stave off cheats, but mostly his exchanges were hand maneuvering and fluid gestures. He'd idle at my street corner with the car window halfway down, under a wide-brim fedora and careful guard. For a long time, his numbers runner was Talent. But she hit the big time pickpocketing, so she passed her position to her teenage grownish-womanish child. When this girl took over, all m'China's bets increased one bob, which she pinched.

As soon as m'China's car came to a stop, Talent's daughter scanned the streets for police before hopping inside. She kept each day's collection between her breasts, like her mother. But being much flatter, the pouch protruded awkwardly through her clothes, as if she was nursing an eager cock with a large comb. m'China would whisper the winning number to her before she fished out the pouch. The girl then got out of his car to signal who scored, galloping through the streets for a horse, twenty-three, or clucking stupidly if it was thirty-one, a chicken. Every number had a sign and sometimes, a winner.

The day Makhadze predicted a penis or death, Ethel kept watch like a hawk, desperate for a sign. Long before sunset, she was peeking out my front windows, eyeing the corner for a car. It was too early. Normally she'd be on her knees scrubbing floors, her plentiful buttocks polishing something stuck in the air. She moved away from the window and got the broom, reaching under the closet and table, collecting yesterday's dust, getting into crevices I always forget tickle. Next she polished furniture—the three-person sofa with crocheted headrest doilies, the scratched dining table they had to unscrew to squeeze through my rear, the mismatched chairs—each made with a different room in mind.

And then the glass cabinet that sealed off the little space in the room. Done dusting, Ethel stood outside. The sun was still high. And really, more cleaning made up her day.

There was a healthy stack of *Drum* magazines to fan artfully so that Miriam Makeba added a pop of yellow to the otherwise dull wood table. There were the doll-size Coca-Cola bottles with fancy red cursive to rinse and display. And Tom's fake gold ash-tray set—a work award for ten years' Anglo-American service, even though Tom didn't smoke—had to be cleaned. After preening my innards, it was time for a bath and some half-hearted gossip, Granny failing to distract her as they both peeled supper's potatoes.

Because Ethel was not the sort of woman to play fahfee, was just the sort gamblers clacked tongues over and called beter koffie—*She thinks she's better than us*—Talent's daughter took a curious and skeptical interest in her bet. m'China's car was still idling when the girl entered Tom's garden.

Talent's grownish and womanish daughter would've seen my public pubic hairs—trim and thick green grass—countless times from the street, but she seemed impressed walking through the verdant smells trapped in my unlikely oasis. And she studied Ethel. And Ethel's reaction. Thank you, my baby, Ethel said, handing the girl an orange. The money was much more than expected. Beginner's luck, Granny scoffed, reminding Ethel in front of Talent's daughter that gambling is for harlots. Thank you, Ethel repeated, a crack in her voice because death won. Number twelve. King would live.

With the money, Ethel decided to finish paying layaway on the children's Christmas clothes early and take pictures while everything was still new. Getting ready took a whole entire week—cleaning every inch of my flat-footed floor bottom and furniture, pressing every collar, trimming every coil of hair, overseeing each shoeshine. Do your father's first, Ethel instructed. Don't make me slap you; those shoes better glow!

On the long-awaited date of the appointment, the photographer was late. That's just like a kaffir, Granny said, folding her arms into a barricade. But she changed her tune after Ngilima arrived, setting up his large floodlights and shiny umbrellas in the front room behind my hearth—my heart chamber. They won't bring bad luck, Ngilima promised with a grin. Granny still refused to pose in pictures paid for with devil money, but she conceded the silver umbrellas had to be good luck. The white man thinks of everything, she said.

Ngilima directed them. Ethel and Granny on either side of the three-person sofa—Ngilima having finally charmed Granny into frame, with peppers of unintelligible English Granny did not understand but still found impressive. Ethel—wearing black high heels and hot-ironed, egg-white-stiffened hair that still clutched, midair, to the C-wave shape of her curlers—held a small leather handbag primly. She rested her other hand on Tom's shoulder. Tom sat center, wide legged on the sofa and flanked by his children, one on top of the other. Before shooting, Ngilima stepped behind everyone, lifting a large framed print to the wall. It was a painting of someone's chocolate-brown baby with welling eyes and shiny afro curls, her shoulders slumped and with two static tears that could just as well have been birthmarks. He hammered expertly, small pricks I barely felt, mounting the frame.

Everyone was excited.

—One! Two! Three! Ngilima shouted.

The force of the flash stunned. Cheeeeze! everyone hollered. *Everyone* but Granny. She stared straight ahead—unmoving—determined not to ruin her first portrait. They made two more. Ethel standing behind Tom, Tom sitting at the dining table, a serious book in his hand. The radio was placed in the foreground, but low enough to still see Tom. Then one more of Ethel reclined across the sofa with a faraway look, the same look as *Drum* magazine's back-page-babes sitting on beachy sand, listening to the sea.

When Simon Ngilima returned, the film developed, Tom was dead. Granny sat with Ethel on the mourner's mattress. King and Tom's brothers saw to everything, choosing a photo from Ngilima for the *Bantu World* announcement. Carefully storing extra copies in the front room, at the back of the glass display cabinet:

> *Tom, né Welcome Mbukeni Thembeka wa Fakude of 7678B Old Potchefstroom Road Diepkloof Zone 6 Soweto died last week on Sunday June 17, 1973. Survived by mother, 8 childrens and wife. Attended Lovedale High School, to Form VIII. Once shook hands with H.R.H. Queen Elizabeth II. Service begins 8:30 A.M., Moroka Parish. Hearse will leave for Nancefield Cemetery 8:00 A.M. sharp.*

After thirty days, most of the relatives left. Everything was quiet with a brooding calm. Ethel rose to make tea. She sat back down with a cutout copy of Tom's funeral announcement and their family album. She looked at the photos. The radio in one picture commanded the shot. It was ugly. Ethel concentrated on her broad smile and the dull ache in her dimples that day. She took the photo out of its casing. Brushed a lint dust from Tom's big nose. He was very black in the photo. Blacker than remembered. And something else. He wasn't looking at Ngilima in any of the photos. Tom held himself with a private preserve. He only looked at Ethel, even when she wasn't in frame. She put the picture back in the album book. Tried to swallow strong tea.

And then they came. Riding hippos. It was a Monday. The hippos were armed with five soldiers apiece—guns at the ready.

Parked at m'China's corner, scraping Tom's hydrangea hedge. Imposing, these hippos. Cast long shadows over mine. Tom's little he-man, his bearded garden gnome, looked infantile and lost, surrounded by all ten white soldiers. They had a helicopter also, hovering overhead. I can still hear the chopper's wings clipping the air into fury. And see people across Old Potch Road, scurrying behind fences. Gawking. I can see them standing behind their gates, parting curtains, peering out, softly clicking and clucking dead tongues.

And then the soldiers scale my walls, stomp onto the asbestos-roof-space that is my crown. Spray a big X, in shouting red letters, across this crown. Next, my innards are guttered: Tom and Ethel's bed. The kitchen cabinets and round-bottomed kettle. The old gramophone. New radio. Everything thrown out, into a low lonely mountain. The soldiers struggle with the dining table, just as Tom had. Finally, they hack down its legs and stack its wood at the gate, blocking my garden path.

Ethel does not resist. She doesn't even read their note. She already knows. She'd tried convincing the Rent Office man who came by to serve notice.

—I have money, she'd begged.

—My son, he'll find work.

—Asseblief, she'd begged. Please, my Baas!

—Next week, my son will have dompass. You come please check us next week.

But the councilman was firm.

—No, Mrs. Fakude. I'm very sorry but you cannot expect us to break the law every time a native is stabbed. In this country, the law is the law. We cannot have a widow as head of household when you are not even a citizen. You must go back to where you people come from. It says here you are Xhosa. So Transkei, isn't it?

—Look. I'm very sorry about your husband, but there's a very long list of qualified natives. Men with proper employment and their families, you understand? Ek is baie sorry, the councilman said.

In my living memory of that Monday, Granny does not stop her wailing. She is not loud, but her body keens back and forth, back and forth. Her now grownish and womanish granddaughter—whom Granny carried from the place where they were forcibly removed, where they were herded out in cattle lorries—that now-womanish granddaughter now unsways Granny, now wraps a plaid blanket around Granny's shoulders.

The hippo's rubber tires are very big. And wide—the whole street needed to clear way for their passage. All of Soweto's dust stirs in the hippo's wake and settles on their things. Ethel teeters through strewn furniture, toward the front-room cabinet. A cut in its shattered glass makes it look like diamond water has sprinkled everywhere. She slides the cabinet's door open. Her pink teacups with English roses survived the move. The fake gold Anglo-American ashtrays also. Ethel reaches beyond these things, pulling out the photo album. Inside, Tom sits at the proud dining table, reading a book. Granny glares ahead, beyond the moment. Afraid to blink. Ethel rips out the photo, buries it firmly inside her breast.

# *Indians Can't Fly*

*The blue of the water was a bright electric hue.*

It made sounds: clapping rain sounds, trickling ice sounds, running water; water running . . . rushing in cold waves and against river rhythm.

*Splash!* Spumes exploded. Spit spray. Water breaking on the ceiling shore. The waves blocking out cries from the hose welting rubber into her back, hoarse shouting rattling something free deep inside her ear. The water blocked out the barking. Six policemen with toad screams and erect dog ears howling right into her ears, shooting spittle straight inside:

—Jy sal kak, Girlie! The fat one farted.

—Where is Jappie?

—Where's your Boesman?

—Sies! Four Eyes spat.

—What would your father say? You fokken motherwhore!

She felt thunder fill the room, but couldn't hear Colonel McPherson and his men. She was swimming in the ceiling.

The water was warm. Sweet. There was no salt in her mouth from her broken nose bleeding and pores sweating and skin swelling. She had never swum in any ocean. How could it come so easy? Buoyed by big waves. Floating above the swaying room and seeing herself a speck or a spore somewhere down below—

suspended between two chairs, hanging like a lemur snatched from the wilderness. A human helicopter.

She didn't need that swinging body to swim. Still, she felt the water parting under her pressure, and because she wasn't wearing anything, because they kept her unshod on a gleaming cement floor in that naked room, she was tickled by air bubbles swimming in and out of her, as though another ocean lay corked between her legs. The water was endless. A faraway shoreline. She stroked her arms out and wide like a peacock fanning its feathers. The water made a snowman of her ripples. She was swimming in a daydream. From somewhere beyond seashore came sonic echoes, faint dispatches from a distant land:

—We know everything, they said.

—Everything     Everything   Everything

And Everyone is *talking*

Talking

Talking

Talking

They ratting you out

Talking

Talking

Talking

She closed her eyes and swam deeper, to the sea floor. From far, weeping willows swayed with the current. A dense forest of fir firmly rooted, swinging to and fro. Forward and backward. Swaying. Gently. So gracefully. Like little playthings dancing with the wind.

As she swam closer, the sea thicket thinned. Those faraway willows revealed themselves: amputated arms with missing forearms and fingers. The playful trees were old men with wispy beards and severed front parts—nothing to cover themselves. She thought she recognized a long dead comrade among the floating forms. Swimming toward her. A growth of strange people carpeted the ceiling sea. Their weight pressed upon her until the forest was dense again and everywhere around her: water. Water everywhere. Choking. Forcing pressure up her nostrils, injecting a sharp sting to her brain.

She could not swim. Since she was a little girl reared on aubergine curries and the bright scent of sugarcane, Krishna could not swim. When she opened her eyes, the sea creature that had turned the ceiling into a burning blue—a violent rush of white waves in which an ocean sprouted, in which she felt herself swimming—was gone.

The floor was cold. Cement, perfectly poured. Her single black braid coiled on the hospital-friendly concrete like a serpent charm. Everything sterile. Shiny. A rubbish bag rustled around her head. It suffocated her screams. Water rushed forward, pressed by firm hands against her face, held tightly in by the plastic hood. So that the water found her open nostrils and screaming mouth. This time, she could hear herself. There was no ocean sound. Her ceiling-sea, gone.

Krishna sang every song in her body. Gauhar Jaan songs she'd hated growing up. *Hanuman Chalisa* verses Ammachchi pinched her into singing. And Brenda Fassie *Zola Budd*. And Queen, again and again: *Save me, Killer Queen*.

When her throat grew hoarse on every chant and lyric she remembered, the thing she tried to muffle washed up afresh:
—What you tell them that for?

—*What!?!* What did I say?

—About Jappie. You told them about Jappie. And Suliman. You nodded at their photos.

—But I said nothing.

—Right! Didn't have to. They have eyes and ears everywhere. They know everything.

—Really? You *really* believe that?

—How else they put it together so fast? About you and Jappie?

—Someone must've told them.

—Someone like who?

—Suliman? Jappie? No. But not Jappie. He's in Africa now.

—So Suliman. *He's* talking. Everyone's talking. And now this Jappie . . . Poof—gone!

—What are you trying to say?

—Be reasonable, Krish. Give them something. *Anything.* A small bone. It's been three days already.

—*Three?* What you mean *three?* I crossed off seven. Look, here . . .

—Does it matter? Don't be stupid, Krish. You want to be the next Indian who couldn't fly out of the tenth floor?

—No! They would never do that! I know nothing.

—And what? Ahmed Timol knew something? Everyone else who fell out of that window or slipped on some soap or drowned in the toilet knew something? Wake up, Krish. You better start thinking. Think of something.

—Like what?

—Like Jappie. Where's Jappie? This whole revolutionary act was *his* fucking thing. And I warned you. Now where is he?

—Shut up! Krishna screamed, out loud, for the whole John Vorster Square to hear

—J U S T! S H U T! UP!

She shut her eyes to block the voice. To drown it. To hum a hymn that swelled the cell.

The flat was quiet when she returned even though signs of a raid betrayed the room. But she found the spilled bookcase and torn pages anchored her. Somehow, the human remains of McPherson and his men in the room—red hair in a teacup and handprints on the window—somehow this tethered her to the cold cleanliness of that cell; to its sterile wall color of young grass sprouting poison leaves. She wanted so desperately to erase its taste and feel but knew its memory bound her, in some irrevocable way she couldn't explain, to Jappie.

She stood with her back to the window and yanked the curtains down. She'd made them by hand. They'd needed something to cover the windows, and why not Amachchi's sari? She clutched the silk to her nose and, smelling the spritz Jappie sprayed into his afro, tasting the cardamom she'd milked into their last chai together, she wept.

The flat was not safe. Tarred. Like the darkening sky. She felt a heavy fatigue demand her. It seemed to sap the fiber of her blood and extinguish every electric current in her mind. She shut her eyes to use the last of her strength to tug the second curtain free. The sari had always been frail, with loose silk threads along its seams and a dull yellowing where the sun washed out the dye. It puddled around her like a moat. She slept in its softness. Below the bare window, facing the door and empty mattress. McPherson's men had stabbed the bed's gut open. Its vomit was a cotton-flower-looking foam the color of beach sand.

At Grootboom's, there were cold beers and peanuts on the small coffee table. Plus a two-liter Fanta Orange for

Krishna. Nobody touched the nuts. The men clutched their beers, the lagers' froth fizzing into soured water. There was also the strong smell of meat losing muscle in the kitchen. Krish knew from before that there'd be a small pot of greens and mashed potatoes for her on the only other burner, maybe also pumpkin with brown sugar and butter. Picturing the food filling a plate made Krishna belch involuntarily. It was a low and ugly sound, different from the high gas burped from a fizzy drink. She covered her mouth and lowered her eyes but the others kept talking without pause.

It was the home of Phelonious Grootboom and his wife. She was a chatty woman whose conversation seldom drew Krishna in. And Phelonious was now—as ever—talking. He was a top editor where Jappie jobbed now and then, *The World*. She'd teased Jappie about that name. What world? she'd asked. How can a narrow regional tabloid claim itself *The World*?

—If we don't provide full coverage, we are culpable.

Phelonious straightened his tie as he spoke. It was a hot Saturday afternoon but the man was dressed in his full Monday morning uniform. Shoes gleaming and cuff links ivory.

—But Grootboom, Zakes responded. This full coverage business is costing us lives. Your whole Current Affairs department is rotting in John Vorster Square. *Right now.*

Zakes tapped his beer bottle against the table, making his point.

—Or they're playing black mampatile with BOSS—where do you think all this hide-and-seek from apartheid's gestapo will lead? When does this kak stop? You know it's just a matter of time before their next roundup . . .

—So we must just sit on our hands because you're afraid to go to jail? Ehn Zakes?

Mosela was speaking now:

—We must just sit like nesting hens. Afraid? Even though we know we'll be arrested anyways. Your grand plan is, Let's sit with our tails tucked between our legs? Like little schoolgirls?

Mosela always sided with Phelonious. Jappie called him *Yebo Baas* behind his back. Everyone else called him Mos.

Krish looked away from the men and the smoke rising with their temperature. Phelonious' wife would be in any moment now with a deep dish of soapy water and a cloth for Phelonious' guests to wash their hands. She'd kneel beside Krish last, *after* serving the men. Krish was tempted to get up and feign playing help. This conversation was a haggard spiderweb: once caught in its tentacles, there was little escape.

She took in the room. The cream crocheted doilies covering the maroon sofa's headrests. Phelonious splayed out on the sofa, manning enough room for three. The wood dining room chairs crowded around the low coffee table; how high they seemed to sit above the Fanta Orange and Castle Lagers. The spent stumps and stuffed ashtrays. And then the leafy plants standing on repurposed Coca-Cola crates, straddling the record player. Phelonious' wife nursed the plants. She once told Krish, responding to a compliment, that the secret to healthy houseplants was furniture spray. She polished and rubbed them down the same way she did her dining chairs. The plants gleamed unnaturally.

Krish had been here only a handful of times. And always with Jappie. Jappie! Where was Jappie now? She'd come to Phelo's to suss this out.

There'd always been the eventuality of exile. Traveling from Jo'Burg to friends in Mamelodi wouldn't've raised much suspicion. From Mamelodi, he could easily claim himself another migrant, heading home to Mmabatho. And from Mmabatho, Botswana could be taken by foot. If Jappie made it that far, freedom lay beyond. Waiting.

She imagined that broad northern swath of backwardness her parents warned against, and thought of Jappie's afro bobbing along its open street markets and mangled jungles like a disco ball flashing light. Zambia, Zimbabwe, Tanzania, Angola— these names promised something but she couldn't say exactly what, couldn't penetrate their meaning on a map or see their precise intersections as real corners where people gathered and gossiped and traffic slowed. She couldn't hear their neighborhood sounds—a salesman's song or a housewife's haggle. The names were emptied of mooring. She grasped none of the People's Power Jappie's pamphlets advertised, clutched from these lands.

—So, Phelonious grinned.

—My sister. You are now officially part of the struggle, ehn?

Krishna squirmed, Phelo regarding her. She tried to smile, to disguise the wreck of her broken nose and tender bruises, but the suffocating smell of food made the effort harder.

—It's sink or swim after Special Branch baptizes you, isn't it?

Nobody responded. Phelonious seemed the only one who found himself funny.

—So you want to follow Jappie? he asked. Does anyone know your intentions?

Krishna nodded, followed by shaking her head no.

—Good. I'll sort you out myself. We have a trusty contact heading to Mmabatho tomorrow. Tonight you'll stay at our safe house. Not far. Mos will take you.

His wife came in, clearing the ashtrays and pouring more beer. Everyone clinked glasses. Krishna lifted her Fanta Orange but was disturbed by the high-pitched clap the glasses made, kissing.

—Cheers! Phelonious grinned.

The men crowded around Krishna with raised arms and threatening shadows.

—Cheers! they barked back, in unison.

The tinkle and chime of their glasses clinking lingered in Krishna's ear and pierced a siren song. She heard McPherson talking to her:

—Would you like a cigarette? McPherson asked, suddenly standing too close.

She *could* use a smoke. She shook her head no, but he'd already stuffed a fresh one between her lips. Reflexively, she cocked her head toward him, leaning her body in to draw his fire.

—Feels good, ne? he asked.

She only inhaled. Deeply. Deeper than a single breath could bear.

—Thanks, she exhaled.

McPherson turned away from her. To a small desk in the corner. There were only a few papers on it. Very neatly stacked. And something cylindrical holding pencils. An old Koo can maybe, with wild freely formed scribble tacked to its ribbed belly. Somewhere in the world, beyond these walls, a child was growing tall and drawing portraits of McPherson in purple crayon and yellow polka dots. He pulled out a chair and gestured to Krish with his hand. He sat on the other side of the desk. Krishna was shaking. Her hair had thinned but she swept it forward. Its stickiness covering her nipples. She crossed her bare legs. Her body—loose grains of sand—shuddering with invisible wind.

—Krish.

McPherson stroked her skin with his eyes.

—The thing about you is, you're a good girl. Aren't you? I can tell.

Krishna pulled herself more tightly in, wondering if her exposed body was saying things she wasn't.

—And the thing about this country is, there aren't enough good volk, you know? Trust me. In my line of work, I see every sort.

McPherson leaned back in his chair now, one leg folded across the other into the number four.

—And look. I'm not saying *we're* innocents.

He motioned at *we* with his smoke—a wand waved for emphasis.

—But the thing you have to understand is that *we* are the ones keeping the law. *Someone* has to be the law. And what we're doing is holding things together. For everyone. The blacks. The Coloreds. Europeans, Indians. *Everyone.*

—You're not stupid, Krish. You've seen the mayhem, the protests. They burn their own schools to smite *us*! What kind of black power is that? They even burn their own! We got more blacks dying from black on black in this country than from anything else. Believe you me!

McPherson's voice flooded with feeling, but his face registered nothing. As if he spoke from a separate, unseen self. He got up, rounding the table.

—Who's going to keep the order? You understand?

Krishna trained her eyes straight ahead, as if McPherson were still seated opposite. She felt the weight of his being fill the cramped hold. He stood behind her, still preaching, then finally sat down. Next to her. Dragging the chair from behind the desk, scraping the floor, positioning himself close, so close she could feel the words escape his breath.

—Look at you, he purred.

—A good girl. From a good family. A *Indian* girl . . . You can't tell me you don't see these commies is just using you?

The shaking hadn't stopped when McPherson spoke from the other side of the desk, but at least her cigarette hadn't been gyrating stupidly between her fingers. She tried to steady herself, tilting her body away from his. McPherson edged forward, subtly, almost imperceptibly, but for the broad chest and shoulders that crowded her space without touch. A near graceful move. Her cigarette dropped to the floor. Krishna could no longer hold her

own hands in her lap, much less the smoke. Her fingers turned
into quake scales, shaking with sudden heat. McPherson reached
his whole torso over, past her breasts and tender belly flesh that
was smooth and soft, suggesting skin unruffled by silver stretch
marks. He bent his body, so agile, just nearly brushing her sweaty
hair, just nearly grazing her nipples. He picked up her fallen cigarette stompie, flicking off the floor's nonexistent dirt, slipping the
smoke back between Krishna's lips and holding it there with the
care of a wet nurse. All the while, speaking. Soft as breath. As if
he were not feeding her, holding nicotine nectar for her, between
her labored inhalations. As if he were not feeling heat escape her
mouth and cool his fingers.

—How long before they spit you out? Like gum? Hmmn?

—You need to think, Krish. Be reasonable. We could help each
   other. You and me. You're a clever girl. Be reasonable. You and
   me—we both want the same things.

Krishna had tried to lose herself in the fumes, to be like the
smoke—an amorphous and impenetrable white cloud evaporat-
ing into some mysterious essence of dust.

And as she'd willed this, one of McPherson's men had entered
the room without her attention. The redhead. He held two short
glasses in his hands, filled full with whiskey or with brandy
or rum. He'd handed one to McPherson and the two of them
clinked glasses. McPherson, lifting his to Krishna.

—Cheers! McPherson had grinned.

Then he got up. Letting the redhead fling an oversize print
into the now-empty chair beside Krishna.

—Sorry, Krish, McPherson said.

—You'll have to excuse me. The boys take club drinks upstairs
   quite seriously. I have to run. But I leave you in good hands.

McPherson gestured to the redhead—already unbuttoning his
shirt collar, already loosening the thick girth of his stiff neck.

Of course, her eyes followed the trail to the photo now in the chair next to hers. In it, a group of men grinned at her. They stood in a half moon, looking into the moon's shadow, beyond the photograph. Behind them, a long wooden bar and an otherwise empty room. Krishna recognized two of them. There was Four Eyes, or De la Rey as McPherson called him, wearing the same spectacles he was always adjusting. And also the redhead. They were smiling. All of them, showing neat rows of Special Branch teeth and clinking glasses. Friday night at the club. It didn't take long for Krishna to see him. Standing among them, like one of them. His nappy halo giving him fake height, the fresh crease she'd ironed into his bell-bottoms that very morning as sharp as a knife.

—*Jappie*, she mouthed.

Her Jappie. Special Branch agent Jappie Erasmus Basters.

igarette, Krish? Phelonious shook her, lightly.

—Krish, he repeated. Commanding, more than offering, a cigarette.

He held the packet too close to her face, she thought, feeling their eyes on her, seeing their chicken-oiled hands pretend interest in their plates. She was shaking again. The doctor said to expect this for the first three days. Something about her nerves and spinal shock. But today was her seventh night outside.

—We should get moving, Mos said, already on his feet.

The beetroot juice on Krishna's plate ran thoughtlessly into her rice—the white completely erased, soaked in beetblood.

The drive was calming. Mos opened the windows and offered her another smoke. Fresh night air filtered in. She couldn't say how long they'd driven or if it was sleep she'd dozed into, but when the car stopped, her head felt clearer, her shaking soft, like the internal vibration of a low hum. There was nothing she recognized around her, except that they were still in Soweto, and that night had grown thick. Mos killed the ignition but they remained sitting in the car. Krishna questioned her sanity—alone in the dead of night with a man Jappie scarcely trusted, *Yebo Baas,* Jappie called Mos. But wasn't Jappie himself an askari? What should she make of anything he'd told her? And yet. Was it wise, putting herself at the mercy of Mos' lead in a labyrinth place she couldn't unpuzzle?

She used the silence to catalogue Mos, to unpack what little she remembered of him. A preacher's son. Strike Number One, Jappie would say. An educated man. You mean for a kaffir, Jappie would add. Mosotho, from the mountain Kingdom of Lesotho. A nationalist: Africa for the African. A rumored Communist. How does an Africanist have so many Russians squatting in his head? Jappie had mocked.

Mos once snuck onto a sugar farm, not far from Krishna's birthplace, and exposed an open secret about what was really sweetening Natal's sugar fields. Six-, five- and nine-year-olds working the farms. He'd estimated their ages. Most of them born into sugarbush, no record of their existence. All of them forced fieldhands. He did a brief stint when those photos made the lead story in *Drum.* Detention without trial. For questioning.

—This is my sister's house, Mos finally spoke.

—Oh, Krish sighed, relieved.

—So Bra Phelo's safe house is your sister's then? Krish asked.

Mos turned from the steering wheel to look at her. It was a studied look, searching, as if weighing the veracity of what lay beyond his viewfinder. Even under cover of dark, it made Krish uncomfortable. The engine, long idle, suddenly stopped humming.

—Krishna, he began.

—Look, Krish. There's some things it's better you don't know.

The shaking again, and the promise of brain pain concentrating now gifted her. She reached for another cigarette.

—There's things that just don't add up. Why did Special Branch come after you? We've all had snafus with them. All of *The World*. But . . . never our wives.

Krish did not know what to feel. Where was Jappie when she needed him most? She didn't even register being called his wife.

—I want you to stay with my sister. Until things shake out. She won't ask any questions and no one knows to look for you here.

—And Phelonious?

Mos looked away. What was he hiding?

—Well . . . Mos began, halting. That's just the thing. I can't prove it, but I have every reason to believe Jappie was *at* Bra Phelo's safe house. Before being disappeared, I mean. Phelo's place is exposed, Krish . . . so . . . Phelonious? I just don't know about Bra Phelo.

They parked the car two streets over, Mos leading Krishna into the blooming dark. She could make out figures here and there, people rushing through the street, the many rows of identical houses—a low fence lining one property, a lone deserted tree hovering over another. And she could hear a dog bark loud from someone's yard. Mos' sister's house was a neat matchbox with two large windows facing the road, a small stoep at the mouth of her kitchen backdoor.

The sister turned out to be Mos' mother's brother's wife. An old woman who lost her husband young but remained close to her husband's family. Mos called her veldskoeMme.

Dumela Ousie Mme, Krishna greeted her the next day, asking how she could help around the house. But the old woman just laughed, seemingly so amused she didn't worry about her gummy grin, didn't laugh with sealed lips, the way Krishna's ammachchi, her grandmother, laughed. But with mouth wide open—her two front teeth guarding an otherwise gaping canyon. After two cups of loose-leaf rooibos with frothy milk and thick slices of leftover sweet potatoes, Krishna finally understood the relation.

—You see that one? Ousie Mme began, pointing to the emptiness that had swallowed Mos.

—That one is my late husband's son.

—Yes, Auntie. Krish nodded.

—So you're Mos' stepmother? Krishna asked.

—No! The fenceless canyon opened, Ousie Mme laughing so heartily Krish felt her own face widen.

—No, no, no! Mosela is my late husband's son. Because Mosela's mother is my late
husband's sister.

—Ahhh! Mos' mom? And your husband? Brother and sister?

—Yesss! A victory clap.

—Yes! Now you see. So when Mosela looked at my late husband, he was looking at
his maternal father.

—Mnh? Krish laughed, confused.

—Yes! And when he sees me, he sees another mother. That's why he's calling me Mme—Mother. And then older sister, Ousie. So Ousie Mme. It started when he was too small, this name.

Krishna finished her tea. The potatoes' buttercream sweetness lingered on her tongue. It was the first solid thing she'd eaten since before.

—Yes, Auntie, Krishna said, smiling.

—Ousie Mme Auntie, Krishna added.

The two women laughed like little girls sharing something soft and sticky and sweet.

Slowly, in that first month after release, Krishna's senses

unclogged to the masked memory of breathing. First came taste, silently restoring her tongue, like rushing water flushing fresh-cut flowers. Next, a lightness returned to her limbs. She found she could stand long enough to wash their dinner dishes. Then she could do a little more, until she was carrying in Ousie Mme's large water bucket from the outside tap without spilling everywhere.

The fatigue sloughed like a slug, leaving a knotty fist of worry in the pit of her stomach. She carried that worry like a woman with child. Nursing its hunger—listening after quiet footsteps, keeping doors shut, never venturing beyond Ousie Mme's back-yard. Imagining the worry alive—was Jappie lying facedown somewhere, a bullet in his head? Should she really trust Mos and the things he said? Maybe that picture of Jappie jolling with McPherson and Special Branch was a lie? Maybe they staged it? Was Jappie really an agent of apartheid? Did *he* send the red-head? She prayed, clasping this worry like mala beads, skinning its hide in sacrifice. Repudiating its grip then embracing it. And as the fatigue wore off, the worry seemed to swell her belly. Jappie became the very name of her fear.

Six weeks out and Mos returned. Early. So early he woke the birds, who sang a determined dawn chorus calling him into their flock. He returned with news. Forty-two days and still no Jap-pie. He was now a wanted person. By the state, officially; and by the movement, quietly. Mos learned through back channels and bribes that Jappie was in fact part of a high-command detail the movement had sent in, in response to Sharpeville, clandestine units deployed to burn Boer crops and bomb their power plants. That was seven years ago, 1961. Jappie—Danny "Schoolboy" Gri-qua to the movement—had been incommunicado since early '63. The movement's attention was swallowed by the Rivonia Treason Trial the whole of '63. But even after, when the few remaining were forced underground or into exile, nothing from Comrade

Schoolboy. If not dead, he'd turned. That's what Mos was told. There was news of Suliman also.

—He got out, Mos said.

—After you. But it's bad with Suliman. Very bad. He's not talking, Krish. They wiped that man away. Whatever's left, it's not Suliman.

Still, Suliman confirmed Jappie was with him at Phelonious' the night one of them got arrested and the other disappeared.

Krishna took in Mos' news. She thought of their flat for whatever reason, a gentle breeze blowing the curtains into kites, late lazy light flooding inside.

Everything was normal. Like before. The evening call to prayer wailed in a distance that echoed also of chanting frogs and the newspaper boy singing the same song he'd sing tomorrow, no matter the world's news.

She saw Jappie. He was sitting on the bed the way they did when people came over. Smoking. A Sunday languor in how he held the cigarette, how he suckled the tobacco and allowed the ash to grow fat and long at the tip of his smoke. Without words, Krish motioned to the walls that weren't the color of their flat, but another color she could feel more than name. Young grass growing in spring. Poison grass. Jappie smiled, responding. A new smile Krishna had never known.

Suliman died the day before Mos fetched her. Heart failure. It was night when Mos arrived. They were already asleep but Krish felt something strange move inside her. *Jappie.* Mos waited till daybreak for Krishna to gather her things and say goodbye. Ousie Mme Auntie kissed her. It was the last time she saw either one of them.

≫ ≫ ≻ ≺ ≪ ≪

S he was already showing when her parents convinced Naicker. He was a trader from nowhere; an unknown nobody whose uncertain caste made him an expensive gamble to any other family. When it came, its starwhite skin pleased black-as-blue Naicker and confounded rumors about Krishna—about how she'd known strange men, about how a Colored (of everything!) had fathered her shame. Naicker named the baby Amra. Amra Naicker.

The milk bottle's nipple was too large for baby Amra, who came too quick and gained weight too slow, so Krishna fed her through tiny openings pierced with a needle into plastic sandwich bags. Nothing about this child was hers. Besides fairer skin, Amra was also born with long slender fingers that seemed to reach beyond her small shadow. Her hair grew thick in curly waves. No one remembered a baby with more hair. And no one seemed to have anything else to say than how strange it was, the bright red bush sprouting like wildfire on Amra's head.

Amra asked only to be fed, burped, changed and bathed. It was from Krishna's grandmother, Krishna's ammachchi, that Amra knew the sound of her own name, the tickle of a shared laugh. It was also Ammachchi who sang for Amra, the same songs Krishna had soothed herself singing in that cell, after a whole ocean abandoned her. But there was one song, Krishna thought, catching Ammachchi's coo, that I haven't heard since I was four. I'd repeat it with childish innocence. Ammachchi would look at me with her faraway eyes that long ago refused to cross the Indian Ocean with the rest of her body. She'd smile and kiss my forehead, but always, after, found something else to sing, forgot which song I meant or switched games entirely. Until I forgot the tune myself, but not the feeling of the song—the long string of loneliness unspooling from Ammachchi's throat.

I don't care to hear it now. My body understands its meaning the way hidden moons know the night. I wonder, why does an old woman sing such a song to a child? Did Ammachchi's grandmother also torture her with this song?

I used to picture Ammachchi coming here, so young. And alone. Worse off, a woman. I used to picture her boarding that ship in Kolkata. The *Jason*. She knew how to say it in English, even if her idea of the thing and its actual sound were as far apart as Durban from Kolkata.

Her emigration certificate from that trip is the only thing Ammachchi still has from India. A piece of paper with her name and her father's name, the way the names would've sounded to a low-ranking British clerk, himself just grasping the spelling of ordinary things like "apel" and "sahree."

He must've guessed her age. Not by asking the girl in front of him, but by imagining what her tender breasts told. Fifteen, he scribbled. There was also room for her caste and kin, her village and who she was married to. Ammachchi's certificate—or the young British officer—say that the girl was unmarried and from a village near Kolkata. But Ammachchi remembers boarding the *Jason* with heavy wedding bangles. And the husband? I've asked. They burned everything we had at Port Natal, she'd tell me, skipping over my question. *Everything.* Cholera. Then they gave us white cotton saris and this paper with our names and colonial number. Which she still knows only in English. And by heart. One. Eight. Three. Two. Four. Nine.

The young Brit must have seen hundreds like Ammachchi. Turned away scores. So what was it about this one girl that tempted him? Her henna, maybe? Telling him that she'd already been had, that his markings would go undetected—that she might even like it. Or was it the clapping-chatter of her endless bangles that excited him, their unbroken song cheering him on as he pinned Ammachchi down? *Manli hands*, he wrote under the Notes section of her certificate: *183249. Ilitarite Coolie girl. Manli hands.*

I said all of this one time, to Jappie. It was after we made love. After one of his endless trips. I never asked Jappie about those trips. Or questioned his evasive answers. *The struggle demands sacrifices*—that was Jappie's favorite line returning from unknown missions, from unpeopled places with nameless men and unsayable stories, "for your own protection," as he'd always say.

What was it about *me* that willed me to believe Jappie's lies? What was it that made me draw the curtains Ammachchi's sari became and undress, in response to those lies? I'd swallow him. My hair back then was long and I'd loosen it into a feral blanket around us as I sank myself low, straddling Jappie, my lips' fleshy muscles clamming around his thick throatshaft like steel clamps. We'd tell stories after, about make-believe places and who we'd be if we could come back to earth as a goat or a bird or a bubble fish.

—One eight three two four nine, I said, giving Jappie the whole backstory.

—Oh, he responded.

—But swannetjie, you know you can't rape your own slave? And that your ammachachi was basically a Brit-branded slave?

That word cut deep. Caught something swimming in the bloodstream of my memory. We were *not* slaves, we told ourselves. *Could not* be slaves. Not like them. We weren't kaffirs, after all; we were better than that. *Better than them*—God! Where did *that* come from?

I know now why Jappie cut deeper than diamonds, why the sheen of that word—slave—had all the dull brilliance of a rough coveted stone mired in dirt: because it's true. *We were slaves.* No better than them. Maybe even worse. After he said this, I was angry. But really, I was angry with myself. What else did I believe that was premised on a lie? That one simple truth shattered me open. I couldn't go back to pretending. I started to see things for what they really were.

Even Jappie, who inadvertently opened my eyes. How he leaned on certain words—*The movement. The people. The struggle.* How I felt his unspoken uncertainty in my body—his returns hungrier, angrier—as though gunfire would explode from his girth.

I knew something was off. They beat him, I know that. They beat a weak limp into his left leg then gave him anti-clotting medication. His handler survived three heart attacks himself, he was not about to witness a fourth. No martyrdom for Jappie. No front-page splash catching his body from another open window on the tenth floor.

Indians can't fly, they told me. And it's true, we don't fly. But we swim. Oh, how we can swim! Across whole oceans. To faraway lands. Like Ammachchi. My grandmother, who was raped before she learned how to swim. Who believes so fiercely that Amra will pull me out from sea. Will fish me whole, return me to myself the way my mother hunted Ammachchi from troubled waters.

I know he turned. I know he led them to Suliman. Over drinks, maybe. Upstairs at their club. Was he up there? Listening? The redhead handling me? *You can't rape your own slave,* he once said. Or did he turn on them too? *WANTED,* as they declared?

He writes, sometimes. To Miss Krishna Naidoo ℅ Kitty's Studio, Pietermaritzburg. On thin envelopes people send into wars.
—Mos is dead.
—Suliman is dead.
—Bra Phelo exiled.

*My swan,* he writes. My swan! The letters are for Amra, I tell myself. One day she will read them and know her mother was alive. Not imagined. But a real thing. A beating heart and labyrinth mind that tried to hold on to something pure and true. I tried, Amra, Krishna wants to write. To make you out of love.

Krishna wades into the water, the ocean around her neck. Her voice breaks on the waves and clashes with the wind.

—"From the full comes the full," she sings, heading farther into full ocean.

—"Remove the full from the full and what remains?" The water rushes in to swallow her. Still, Krishna keeps singing.

—"What remains?" she sings, salt water stinging her nose.

—"The full."

She never could swim, Krish. Sand sifts and shifts under weight of her body. "From the full comes the full." Her body sways, lilts just so—a volley caught and kicked by playful waves not meaning much harm. Arms, hands and legs liquefying into ocean. This is full, Krishna thinks, the Indian Ocean's whole body shouting prayers over her water-laden lungs.

—I am full.

# Black Christmas

*Christmas was bulldozed. Only the birds weren't told. They* still fly, very bold. Landing like soldiers: everywhere. They are not darkie or mosweo, how we sing at my school, *Two little birds, sitting on a tree. One named Peter, bright white light. The other named Paul, black with spite.* But blue. True blue, a blue that hides in the sky. And red that is dirt after rain.

Mma's sister also wasn't told. Why else she send blind Koko, Mma's Mma, to come to visit us in Soweto for Christmas? Plus her whole bloody Sekhukhune brood? Now we are fourteen in a three room house. Emagine, fourteen! Uncle Fix threaten he build a shotgun shack to grow us space, but that will never happen in Mma's house. You're dreaming, Mma tell him. So now, with everyone alive living in this three room, we are a full soccer stadium sleeping inside the goalie box.

Uncle Fix and his wife, Ousie Dikeledi, they sleep on the sofa. The boys have a sponge in there, in the dining room. Koko use Mma and Ntate's bed. They take the floor. Me and Ousie Portia and Ousie Linda, when they have off, plus the Sekhukhune girls—we all tuck in, very close. We sleep near the stove, under the table. Is not bad. Just hot. Mara this one? The smallest one from Sekhukhune? Eish! She sleep like a bull with blood filling its horns—kicking and shifting, pulling the blanket and speaking funny nonsense, round after round. Mara she stopped wetting the blanket. First night, I told her straight, Try that pisspie here and I'll make you suck it dry every morning. She scare. Big fish eyes flashing, and duck her head into her all-bone knees. Shame. I feel bad after, but you know who must wash those blankets if she not told? I've got enough work. Ousie Portia is the only one she helps me. She feel sorry for me.

Before making it as a kitchengirl in Saxonwold, Ousie Portia was me—she was the Cook, girl! Wash the wash, girl! Clean up, girl! Sweep, girl! Ehn . . . ? Stupid girl! You don't smell that? Change the baby, girl! Ousie Linda, firstborn before Ousie Portia, she left as soon as she could. She fourteen that time, maybe? Her ou find her a job with his Madam. We did not see Linda for forever. Mma losing a lot of weight that time. The veins outside her hands grow fat. Her breath thin. Then Ousie Linda's Madam move and find Linda another Madam with a big-big house. They need two house girls. Linda put Portia in. That's how Ousie Linda she finally come back. Mma so happy.

They are rich, Ousie Linda's new whites. So rich they throw away meat. Every other Thursday, Ousie Linda and Ousie Portia bring us this meat. You cook it in vinegar then chew and chew. Chimps chomping chops, Ntate say, fighting the plumpest piece. Cow meat, sheep meat, even chicken and pig meat. Pork, the box call it. And polltree. Throw away good meat because it is sitting inside a icebox two few-nyana extra days? Emagine!

That same rich Madam give Ousie Portia her daughter's uniform. For Christmas. Little Madam's old school uniform. Ousie tell me little Madam is in Form Five, just like me. Next year, me and little Madam is going to high school. We same age. But her clothes? Tjo! Tjo tjo—so fat! She's a giant, little Madam. I look like I'm from Ethiopia in her dress. The radio say Ethiopia people so hungry you see a man's heart right through his shirt. But the dress is smart. And new for me. And one day is one day. One day, I will eat cheese breakfast, peanut-butter jam sandwich after school and obvious, every single night—I will eat meat. Then I will grow till that dress fit me nice and neat, like a real little madam.

Ousie Portia also buy me a proper jimdress. You are going to high school, she say. You'll be a woman just now-now. You need to dress like umfazi. And how about you shock us, lady? Act like one! Otherwise, she smack her lips, otherwise, you'll never marry. Who will marry you?

Me? I'm not going to marry. I know what happens if you marry: childrens. Like Mma—farming babies how seeds shake from sunflower. No, I say, I don't want to marry. No babies for me. But then I picture Ousie Dikeledi. Three years and still, nothing. Not even a girl. Uncle Fix never say fokol, but Mma not allowing Ousie Dikeledi nowhere near fresh meat or the baby. She cursed, Mma whisper. Ousie Dikeledi never taste even snoek fish since she come to live here.

Me, I say all this and Ousie Portia listen. Smiling sly. What you think you'll do then? Ehn? she ask, join the circus? Or you just gonna steal they donkey and hump its arse, selling coal? Kwaaa! We explode. Emagine me—black, black, black, covered in soot. Knees ashy, face blue black, shouting in my donkey cart: Mala-a-a-a-hle! Mala-a-a-a-hle! Carrying coal sacks how a baby ride motherback. The whole thing just finish us laughing so that me—my mouth hurt like I'm Koko's floating smile in the tall glass at night, next to the breadbox. I feel Koko's rotted teeths inside my mouth, grinning their statue stare.

I don't tell Ousie Portia, but I know what I want to be when I grow up. Mistress Manaka call me a sjupid when I tell her I want to live in a big house with the things Ousie Portia say—a tee-vee with smallanyana people inside, living upside down. A icebox with fresh meat every week. A bed for only me and lots and lots of condensed milk and ultramel, even if it's not Christmas. When I grow up, I want to be one of them: Makgoa.

After I tell Mistress Manaka, she move me to the domkop desk. We are fifty eight in my class, twenty three around the domkop desk. Most of the domkops is not too bad. Well, most. Minus one bone-thick hardhead. Everyone call him s'Gilogo. It mean cross-eye, what we call him, but really his one eye is running away from his good one, like maybe it will one day catch s'Gilogo's shadow. He is just s'gole sa Modimo, s'Gilogo—living proof that God fails also, sometimes. This year s'Gilogo repeat Standard Five for four times straight. Even Mistress Manaka say s'Gilogo would be better off in the guts of a mine somewhere—there is just no hope for that kind of sjupid. Plus his mother she not married and she old. People say she was a schoolteacher also, long time now. Before Bantu Educations. That s'Gilogo born after. I don't know. I don't even know his real name.

One day after Mistress Manaka move me to the domkop desk, s'Gilogo ask I help him. We had a test tomorrow so even if I'm not suppose to, I whisper quick-quick the train station names we cram in s'Gilogo's ear, my hand covering my mouth: *Naledi, Merafe, Ntlanzane, Khwezi, Dube, Mphefeni, Phomolong, Mzimhlope, Mlamlankunzi, Nancefield, Kliptown, Tsiawela, Langlaagte, New Canada, Mayfair, Park Station.*

s'Gilogo stare outside. His crazy eye still stuck inside. He look somewhere—very far outside. Outside the school gate, past the soldiers. Outside the road, where the dirt cake in a puddle. He look outside like the world have no sky. Then he turn and he stare at me. Says the thing Mistress Manaka do to us is poison. Everyday, Bantu Educations is poison. His mother tell him. But she say even though Die Groot Krokodil lock our brains in his jaw, mining is more worse. Testing God that far underground is walking into the sea—water roaring, earth sinking—and never looking back. I wonder where s'Gilogo mother ever see the sea? Where she ever heard a person walk inside a sea?

I was saying it is Christmas. But this year is black Christmas. Comrades come to tell us, door to door—Bang! Bang! Bang! Con-Zoom-R Boycott, I hear them say.

—Another bloody boycott? Papa asking.

—It is the People's Strike, the Comrade say. He is the smiling one, but his eyes make no smiling lines.

—We mourning, Baba! the boy from Caretaker's street add.

—Mourning? Papa make a soft spit sound between his teeth.

—Who is mourning? Papa ask.

—And who are we mourning? The same klevers that bringed us seventy six?

—Our leaders, Baba.

Smiling Comrade still smiling but his words coming out snake slow. Like Mistress Manaka making him spell them out:

—*Our. leaders. in. detention. or. in. the. ground.* There can be no Christmas for our people.

—And what do these boycotts do? Papa sneer. Win us more tanks? You counted all the hippos manning Soweto? Die Groot Kro-kodil's army is camped deep inside your arrr—

—Ahhh! Mma scream.

Koko's rotted teeths glass falling sudden from Mma's hand.

—Sorry, she say, bending to pick up the statue smile.

—Eish! So sorry my son.

Water from the teeths glass spill on the Comrade shoe.

—Clumsy old hands, Mma say, shaking.

—I'm so sorry, she saying it again and again, wiping they shoes, smiling funny and then, standing to face the main Comrade:

—We know now, my son. Don't worry. December sixteen. We stay away.

I'm still not too sure why, but you can't even buy Christmas on layaway. Because Comrades ban festive. Don't wear your new Christmas clothes outside, they strip you naked if they catch. Don't throw a show-off party, your friends singing Hip! Hip! Hooray! Comrades stone your windows and make you watch from inside. And don't even think about the weekend. STAY AWAY, Comrades paint it on Orlando Stadium walls.

I think maybe the Comrades must be chicken shit Pirates. I mean, why—after we beat them 4–0—why all of a sudden, no Christmas match to show Orlando Pirates the real number one boss of Soweto? Ehn? But we will show them, shame. Chiefs will moer Pirates after Christmas. Watch! But the worse of all, because of this strike, we don't do music, like choir competition at Church and drum majorettes on Saturdays. That one kill me. What kind of Christmas we make without even drum majors singing the streets alive?

I say this to Uncle Fix. He smile. Make your own music, he say. So the boys make guitars with paraffin empties. Uncle Fix appear with a whistle out of nowhere and the one from Sekhukhune blow it out of tune. We steal Mma's dithlwathlwadi seed pods and fix them so my feets rattle when I walking. I sing. We call ourself Butterfly Sting. I love Ali and how he always name hisself funny names that Uncle Fix shout when he drinking, Floating in a Butterfly, he say, Sting like a Bee. I like that. We sing a lot of songs we make ourself. I can't remember them now. And also we sing the Jackson Five, the Commodores and Gladys Knight. Me, I'm Gladys Knight. The boys my Pips.

I am like a Black American the time I sing. I even get Ousie Portia to do me *Black Like Me* hair, but it come out only one side. She say the perm needs to stay more next time. Until it burn. What!?! What next time? My scalp already Kentucky Fry *this* time. I don't think so. She is dreaming, Ousie Portia. I can act Black American without *Black Like Me*.

We practice. Every day, we dance after I finish cleaning, sing as I busy cooking or soaping dishes or hanging the washing. Even Uncle Fix, he say, You bliksems sounding good. Until one day, one of the boys' friends call him impimpi. Snitch, the friend spit. They get in a big fight and the friend klop him on the head with the guitar, bending the paraffin box so the strings come off. Everything kaput after that. The boys don't want they call them impimpi. So Butterfly Stinging is finish and klaar. Our new game now, we box. Fight like Ali fight. Tussle with a whale fight, hand-cuff lightning fight—until we called inside to buy three candles and two Rothmans 24, before outside is turn dark.

Everyday, me or the boys buy three candles for Mma, and a cig-arette for Ntate and Uncle Fix also. That's another one. When the Comrades tell us about black Christmas, they say also, No electric-city after seven. Candles Only! I see Mma wanting to laugh. Me too, I almost laugh. There is no electric in all of Soweto. Every-body knows Abuti Phelonious Grootboom house the only house with the electric. At nighttime you see his house from f-a-a-a-r. It glow alone with fat light, like the one star Soweto somehow snatch from the night. People even say he has telephone. I don't believe until one day Uncle Fix send me to Abuti Phelo with Nina Sim-one. She is black American, Nina Simone, mara on the LP cover her lips is Bible-book thick and her hair buried dead in a doek, like the same ones Mma and Koko wear, like maybe she's a Venda fresh from the bush—a real Betty come to Jo'Bek. Shame, this Nina Simone. What kind of black American?

So I take her back. To Abuti Phelonious. And that's when I see it: shiny and black with round white circles inside another circle. Sitting on a small wood table with nice like-lady legs painted at the feets, how Ousie Portia and Linda paint they toes red and Mma pretend she don't see. I know it's a telephone first time I see it. Abuti Phelo ask, Anything else? Eish—I am so embarrass. I am so busy staring and staring I forget myself.

When I grow up, I'm going to have a telephone on a lady table like Abuti Phelo's, with white feets. And I am going to marry a husband like Abuti Phelo—a fat cigar in his teeths and a sparkly glass in his gold watch hand. Scotch on ice, Uncle Fix say.

Uncle Fix and Ntate go to Abuti Phelo house to drink now; now that shebeens must also stay away. Sometimes—late, late at night, I hear Ntate come back from the only shebeen open after the Comrades go to sleep. It is in Orlando, this place. Mma say she hope the Comrades catch Ntate, make him snort that shebeen piss up his nose, or maybe some soldiers pour it in his ears. I hear this late at night, by mistake. I suppose to be sleeping but then I hear Ntate come in, Mma say the thing about his bloody swine shebeen drink and a hard klap later, Mma mute. The house shut up.

I don't like Ntate. He say no one will marry a girl that knows too much, You know too much, he say. Ask too much. A little poofy, he call me. So I ask, what is this poofy?

—What is poofy, Ntate?

—A nincompoop nitwit ninny.

—How is that one, Ntate? A poop neat poofy?

He tell me nothing.

—But Ntate, what is a . . . ?

—Silly girl, he say.

Uncle Fix nicer for me. I steal his newspapers when he fin-ish. I'm not suppose—only suppose to light the stove with stale news, or fire the coal rock with the sport section, or wipe the smallanyana ones' kak with the Backpage Babe. But I don't do what I suppose. I read.

The newspaper put a picture of a terror man in there, a comma-union-its. He's busy bringing danger, even to inside the courtroom, it say. "Tell my people I love them," that's what the newspaper write, "and the struggle continues." The headline read, "Dead Black Commie: Final Words." When I ask Uncle Fix what commie mean, he say this is not things for a little girl. His voice shiver. I hear it. Uncle Fix never anger. I suspect the comma-union a real rot, that's why Uncle Fix blacken. I change the subject. But the newspaper say we now a state of emergency and keep writing this news every day— about terror attack, about failed sabo-tour operations and dangerous black terror men and comma-unions burning innocent blacks.

I know about burning. I never tell. Never tell not no one. I saw a necklace one time. I wet the blanket that night but nobody know. I am the wash girl, remember? It is cold that day, windy. August wind. Ntate send me to buy two Rothmans 24 and only two candles, late. I am try to run fast-fast, because is so cold. Winter raw that night—not a stray dog outside. And smoke everywhere. I take the double-up through the passage to Zone One. To the shops that side. After the passage, there is a s'ganga you pass and behind it, a preschool. That rubbish dump, the s'ganga, usually have a small clearing against the preschool fence.

Before coming out the passage, I smell the burn. It is very thick. Heavy. Pig meat with salt and rot and iron. It could be maybe a braai, but the sweetness fill my mouth with bile when I turn and see a man tied to the preschool fence—a rope around his neck. Black tire where pants should cling. Some Comrades say the fire not big enough for this dog, impimpi. Most silent. Quiet. But the fire talk. Loud. Eat everything. Anything. The man not fighting. The sound swallow his screams.

Statue.

I cannot think. Or leave. Or throw sand in his face. I cannot even cry. I tell no one. Never tell. I mess myself without feeling, until it is cake on my skin. I can't smell it, even when I am home, after. Only one smell inside me. Mma make me wash my legs and hang out the dress. She doesn't say, What happen? What's wrong? Knows something wrong. I sleep early. Forget supper. When I wake tomorrow, I have difficult speaking. That is how Mistress Manaka, she first sit me with the dommest domkops at the dom-kop desk. It is long time before words rename theyself to me.

Seeing Koko, the one she live in Alex, she didn't know language leave my tongue. First thing when I visit her for June holidays, first thing she say is, Where is your *s*? I show her with my shoulders up, so my shoulders touch my ears. Say surreptitious. Koko speak very big English. She is the only person who speak to me isiNgisi like I understand. She's clever. Cleverest in the family. Mma say she went to Lovedale, before Bantu Educations destroyed our schools. And the way Mma say Lovedale, I know there's no domkops in that school.

—Thhh—rrr. . . . tha-rrrap-tish-ya-thie.

She make me say it again, S-l-o-w. I repeat.

—When did *this* start? She frown.

I don't say anything about burning, about the necklace—how they burn that man, how the smoke grow and swallow the night. I pull my shoulders up to hug my ears. She say something about Mma and Ntate in big English, like I understand.

—E Reverend. Paw paz.

I go outside.

Koko live alone. Ntate her only child. The others is dead or disappear. Inside Koko's yard is Baba Mthimkulu and his wives. Two of them. Then there is Ousie Mavis. She is new. Her boy my age, but he wear always new clothes and puts on his mother's pink-hair slippers. Stays shut inside forever. Never coming out and play. I think maybe something is wrong with him. Like maybe he's a girlboy, a weak and wicked s'thabane?

The other families has childrens also. We play together. Kabelo, Nono and Kopano—they stay with their mother, but she is always working. They say sometimes they see their father when she have off. She take them to the mine hostel, far away.

Kopano the middle one. Quiet, most time. But one day he say his father would live here if Koko stamp his dompass so he have permit for Alex; then his father would live here.

—Stop being a sjupid kaffir, I tell him.

—No blacks stamp no bliksem dompass and it's not my granny's fault your father doesn't want you!

We don't play together for a long time after that. But then the toilet pipe break and the tap by the latrine—our whole yard tap—it spray water up. It grow up and up and up, and then come down. We all running in and out the raining tap water until we dizzy from gurgling wet laughs, until we friends again.

Tjo—I am so happy. Because when me and Kabelo and Kopano and Nono is no more friends, I am force to play alone with the Shangaan kids—*Every. Single. Day.* I start to worry. What if they turn me Shangaan too? Them and their mother—always in that puffy motjeka skirt making her bum jive, like maybe she one of Mahlathini's backup singers, like she practicing to be a Mahotella Queens. But jirre, as God kyk my goed! 'sTrue 'sGod—that Shangaan woman can cook. One Sunday she buy two fat chickens on First Avenue and snap them furry necks off, right there, at the tap. She scald the skin and ask we all help pluck-plucking they feathers and gutting grass and grit from they gizzards. After, when she plate those chicks in they own gravy, I am so happy I'm not saying no before, that I don't eat Shangaan food. Because you never eat chicken until you eat Shangaan chicken. Tjo, I'm telling you! And only with pap—'sTrue 'sGod.

A cow doesn't shit everything in one go, Koko say, still asking me, Where is your *s*? I know this saying, but how me and cow shit get mix together? I keep quiet. The very next tomorrow morning, she wake me before the sun. Dark. Alex so quiet. Only scrawny dogs and hairless goats picking through the streets. We walk. You walk everywhere with Koko—that woman never heard the word taxi. But there's no taxis anyway. We're in the end of time for night, not in tomorrow yet.

The windows are undressed at the house where we going. But you can't know this from outside—faded black paint clot out all the light. The man inside sit like he born waiting for us. He have a white curtain hanging in the room's private part, a big tin wash-tub behind this curtain.

—Take everything off, Girl.

This is the man's first words for me, growled in his Mahlatini voice.

—Now, get inside that tub.

I look at Koko. She makes a face—it say, Do like you're told. So I undress my clothes and sit inside the tub. The water not cold. Dark still inside the room, but outside—the sun waking. The man say things to Koko about our ancestors. She speaks with them. Many I don't know. Some she call with my name. Koko know all our ancestors, from before old Chief Thulare even. As she call them—twelve generations gathering in one room—I stare at the water, try to see what the floating brown and gray is. It have a very sharp smell. Some is just leaves, but the graybrown bits is musty. It smell like dead mold mix with the earth taste of fat mopani worms after red rain. I have to concentrate while

Koko talk so I don't put the graybrown on my tongue or sniff it up my nose. Koko almost finish naming us.

Mister Sangoma, he say something, then he stand up. I only see now, after he stand, he wearing nothing. Only a long wrinkle shirt. He make me stand also. And then I feel his hands. Ox hands. How I am taller than a man born one hundred years before me? I smell his hair. It's not smelling like old people. Instead, it's briny, Zam-Buk like. The skin in his hand thick. Many veins on his forearm run in a race—vein chasing vein, bone to bony elbow. His long slim fingers wash me, rain water over my head so many times I scare I will swallow.

I start to shiver everywhere, like when your teeths clatter, until I see how the sun sit inside also now. How is so sudden light. Koko give me a waslap to dry myself. The sangoma fetch more graybrown. He show Koko how to pour it in my tea until the tea drink everything solid—every morning—until my sickness sated on graybrown.

We walk back, silent. Never say nothing about that house and its old man with ox hands. You won't believe but after that one time in Alex, I can say s-s-s-u-r-r-e-p-t-i-t-i-o-u-s like a snake. I find my *s*.

That one was in wintertime. Winter holidays. Is Christmastime now. Christmas holidays. Maybe, because we now fourteen in a three room, Mma will send me back to Alex? Minus one mouth, she will easy say. But instead, Mma send me to town. Ousie Linda and Ousie Portia have not been back since last of last week. That's two Thursdays. That's one month. Mma is sure they dead. Ousie Dikeledi say that's crazy, obvious maRussia kidnap and force them. You know what those Sotho gangs do with pretty girls? she wince.

Mma wake me early. Already she iron my Sunday dress—the one from Ousie Portia's little Madam, the one that make me look like Ethiopia. I also wear my school mary janes. Shine them, quick-quick. Then Mma gets the afrocomb and squash me inside her elephant thigh. She takes out one long center line—part my face into two. Burn scalp into sin the way she sink that comb's teeths in my hair. Pulls. Glycerine help. Hoe and harrow till a fat dead hair mound grow loose in her hand. Till the teeths plow my kaffir hare into silk. Till my hair broke in. She tie a ribbon in each lepondo when her work finish and I am black is beautiful.

The instructions to the place where Ousie Linda and Ousie Portia is kitchengirls is long. Remember the station names? This is why, Mistress Manaka say, you must learn your station names. One day you'll be kitchengirls. No kitchens in Soweto. Madam kitchens is in Jo'Bek. You must catch the train. Remember the stations. Off at Paki. Look for a bus, the right bus. Look for the signs, Non-Whites Only. Sit in your place.

Inside the bus, Jo'Bek pass me. Factory girls getting off they shift. Paper boy singing the day's headlines, the world's news stacked high on his head. No soldiers here. Kitchengirls in they black and white uniform. And ladies. White ladies in white gloves. One day, I promise myself. One day I am going to—I will wear those gloves one day, too. When I become one of them, lekgoa. A shop pass us, red writing shouting the shop name. A big round watch on top of that shop. M-A-R-K-H-A-M-S, the writing say. At the robot, a blue arrow points for Jan Smuts Avenue. When the robot turn green, we follow this arrow.

Trees begin to pass us in place of tall buildings. Worshiping trees. Hands lifted to God how Mma do on Sundays, like maybe God's spare change will find a hole through the sky. The trees is praying. A big prayer. They pray for something so strong God ask for all they power. Houses pass now. Beautiful houses.

—Saxonwold Post Office, the bus driver shout.

I am here now. Quiet. The sound is butterflies and birds. Same birds like we have for Christmas, but they sing songs I never hear at home. A Zulu baba, earlobes stretching to his shoulder, he smiles to me. Lucky, he is not wearing iziqhaza, those Zulu ear plugs that scream, *Me, I'm Jimmy Come to Jo'Bek!*

I show him my paper. He ask what it say. He shake his head no when I say the address name and number; his earlobes jiggling. So I explain Ousie Portia for him.

—Ehn-heh! Portia? He beam.

—Hau! Why didn't you just say? And then he explain:

—You see this street? You go up this street, straight-straight. His arm point forward.

—You see people maybe, sitting there—clever kitchengirls sitting in the sun. Busy gossiping when the white man say work. Don't fool yourself with such people. You just keep, s-s-s-tr-r-r-aight. Again, he stretch his whole arm, hand and fingers.

—Until you pass this house, he say. White elephants guard this house. When their trunks and tusks get behind you, you turn this way, he show me with his right side.

—Follow your eating hand. The place you want is Fanta orange.

At the house, the next-door kitchengirl take me to a back passage and then sudden-sudden, we inside the house, but behind. Tjo—a swimming costume! I wonder if this is how the sea look, the hungry sea s'Gilogo's mother say swallow people the way mines vomit diamonds after eating boys like s'Gilogo. I don't go near to find out. Behind the swimming costume is a small white room. Portia inside.

Tjo! Portia so happy to see me. She look different in her kitchengirl uniform. Funny. Your granny butterscotch shoes, I point, both of us laughing. She say the Madam had a big party last of last week, so no off. She pay R2 extra. *Emagine*–we rrrrich! I tell her Ousie Dikeledi already know which Russia make her his gangster wife. We laugh harder. Then she say, Wait here. She fetching Ousie Linda.

I sit on the bed and lean forward, head between knees, looking under the bed. I see Ousie Portia's shoes and night bucket. I see her still-wet underwear and waslap hanging from a hook under the bed. Dust. A Bible under there too. Bricks, three-by-three at every corner. I am wondering what these bricks is for, if maybe Portia have tokoloshe problems, when I sudden feel someone.

—Hello?

I rise my head too quick. She smell like Abuti Phelo. A garden. A thick too-ripe sweetness. She now standing in the doorway. My eyes drop, but I feel her look. She close. Too close. I dry my hands on Portia's bed. Quick, I think: *Stand!*

At school, Mistress Manaka teach us how you speak to makgoa. We practice, but I never speak with a real Madam before. Or a little Madam, like this one. You suppose you stand. You suppose you don't look straight in they eye. I try remember the thing Mistress Manaka made us cram, in real English:

—Good morning, Madam! My name Maria Molatodi Nkadimeng! I have eleven years of age! My school is baPedi Lower Primary! Eish—sorry . . . my . . . I . . . Me I go to baPedi Ikageng High. School. Ja, I . . . I . . . I going to baPedi High School! My home address in Diepkloof Zone Two. My father Mr. Nkadimeng! He born Alexandra Township! He work. He w-w-work-ing in—

—What are you doing? She cut me, eyes shrinking to narrow folds, laughing.

—What the hell was that? she ask.

I look down, away. I look at Ousie Portia's wardrobe. But little Madam doesn't stop laughing—even while screaming over her shoulder for Portia, she laughing. Even announcing to the whole world:

—We need more tea! She laughing.

Me. I emagine myself—still standing and staring at Ousie

Portia's wardrobe doors. So I sit. Little Madam look at me—eyes unnarrow now, laugh still squeaking from the sides of her talking mouth:

—You look so silly in that dress. Why are you wearing my fucking school uniform?!?

She turns and goes. Hot tears mud my eyes.

The mirror agree. I look silly in her dress. A giant in little Madam school uniform. I am drowning. Ousie Portia is back with Ousie Linda. I make excuses to leave. They give me money. Not tomorrow, but tomorrow's tomorrow, is Christmas. Portia makes sure we have enough for meat, vegetables, baking flour, fresh eggs and a case of Coca-Cola. Tennis biscuits and ultramel if they have them at the Zone One shops. I hide the rands inside my shoe tongue. When I'm outside again, past the swimming costume and out the snaking servant path, I see the tree has been busy also, busy purpling the tall front gate. That laugh. Giant little Madam's laugh still ring in my ear. I look up at the tree, stare it down to its root. I spit. I spit hard at its root.

The train stations pass me again:

Naledi

   Merafe

      Ntlanzane

         Khwezi

        Dube

           Mphefeni

             Phomolong

               Mzimhlope

                 Mlamlankunzi

                   Orlando.

Stations Mistress Manaka teach us in case we lucky—if makgoa make us their kitchengirls and gardenboys.

So many Comrades at Orlando Station. They check our bags

to make sure we stay away. A woman with oily skin explain why she bought a big Omo washing powder box from town and so many grocery in checkers plastics. The Comrades spill the soap on the train track, her groceries after. The oily woman clutch herself, both her hands fold to hold her stomach insides, in case they maybe spill out, also.

—Next time, Mama, the Comrade bark so everyone hear.

—Next time you will eat that soap.

She shaking now, the empty checkers plastic bag the Comrade give back to her crackling in her hand. She hug it into her breast. I don't look at my feet, so no one see our Christmas rands.

We hurry out Orlando Station. Hippos with soldiers with guns and cigarettes in they thin makgoa mouths is filling the street again, coming for curfew. I walk home, a stone in my stomach. I think about what that Comrade said: Next time. Is next year also another black Christmas?

# Star-Colored Tears

*I like it when I am sleeping and then I am awake, then walk* inside my house but it is very big—yet still my house—not ant house like I told Papa and he got mad and said, We have real roof not asbestos, we have running water outside and even a toilet *on the inside* of my house. So, why you say ant house? Do ant house have the electric city? Do ant house have washing sink?

Me, I say nothing. I am shut up and do magic trick where I close my eyes tight-tight-tight, like this, until I am back in there, back inside this very big house where Papa ask if I want more yogurt and I say yes and he is opening a big icebox door and the sun inside the box is shining very bright so you can see there is yogurt on every shelf, inside the icebox door and even on the bottom where it is cold and my feet make me jump so high because cold air is coming so fast, fast like this and it has a low whoozing sound like the feeling my heart thump when the crazy boy up the street fight because we call him s'Gilogo—crosseye.

He is kind of a little dom, you know? But not too-too sjupid, not a real domkop. Because, well, I am not suppose to say, but because one time I see him in the back of our house with my sister and I hear the same sound. You know, like Papa and Mme Zuma, Sfiso's mother, when Papa tells me to wait outside and not be a little shit. To be a man.

Anyways s'Gilogo seen me and I saw him and he stopped and I am thinking, maybe now I start running? But before that I want to shout, Bona! Bona—Malefa le s'Gilogo! Bona—look! But instead I see me becoming like a little shit, not a real man, and s'Gilogo see this also and he come to me and say I better not praat te veel if I know what's what.

After that day I start hating Malefa a little bit inside because why did she just stand there like a mute and let a domkop like s'Gilogo talk to me like that? But I think Malefa must see inside my head because she catch up to my scheme and is nice-nice, so extra, making me love her so that I forget to count how many times I need to hate her for what she did. Soon I forget my plan and just go back to being Malefa's little man, how she call me.

Malefa is the only girl I really love and we have many secrets together. She teaches me naughty things sometimes, but mostly just stuff grownups don't want you to know. Not hanky-panky business these kids do because they think to be grown is to be doing it all the time, these little shit moegies. Like you, ninkumpupie!

I love that word, ninkumpupie. It makes a sound like something you maybe drop from your mouth because it is hot inside from all the sweet potatoes you eat—one and then two and eat and eat some more and then swallow quickly with hot tea because it is morning time on Christmas Day and so you have to eat a lot so you don't miss out and your brothers and sisters finish everything and you miss out because it is Christmas and Christmas is not everyday.

Ninkumpupie is like it dropped out of my mouth from then on. Maybe that's why I like it, because I like Christmas time; even when we don't have new clothes—then I just pick a real moegie showoff with the smartest new clothes and sink my fiercest jokes in him and don't let go all day until the day is over or the moegie cries, just like Bra Mike's rottweiler, Gwaza, when he would not let go of Tsepo's leg the time we jumped the fence and got inside and saw the dog and I jumped right back out and forgot about the peach tree.

And I don't even like peaches. It's just because Sfiso dared me and someone called me chicken when I said I don't even like peaches, so I jumped the fence and said I'd beat the chicken shit out of him when we finished too, but then that Tsepo had to get Gwaza's teeth buried in his leg like a lock and we all forgot about the chicken beating and the peaches.

Bra Mike came to my house and told Mama about Tsepo and I think he was shit scared about Gwaza and Tsepo's bleeding and was saying sorry Mme—ke Sorry. Of course Mama threw me a nthathle without even looking in my direction to show Bra Mike she was sorry too, for raising such a no-good son who jumps into people's yards and that she would be dealing with me after; after Bra Mike finished his tea with our last teaspoon of sugar and the milk I am supposed to be eating with bohobe after; after Bra Mike leaves.

Mama is finished and klaar with me. She send me to bed without even bohobe, but I am so happy she does not tell Papa and she does not really give me a good hiding. I almost kiss Mama before running out. And anyways, Malefa sneaks me masonja before starting to cook but I think it's because she wants to know all the details about Tsepo and Gwaza. Of course she asks if the dog Gwaza said anything before it bit Tsepo because Malefa has some crazy ideas about cat and dog familiars slipping at the last minute and speaking in the very voice of the witch who sent them, right before stealing final breath from a children lung.

She says it's something about a pure spirit and the animal smelling itself in the children fear. Me, I just eat my mopani worms and nod to everything Malefa say so Mama doesn't hear my voice talk-talk-talking and I wait until Mama calls Malefa about the pots on the stove and, Hei wena, Girl! Will this dinner cook itself?

I like it when Mama comes home early and spares us Malefa's five-headed meats and potato meals, followed by Papa's chorus after Malefa's meal about the girl who cooked fish with bohobe and bohobe with lettuce. What is this lettuce? I am asking myself. Even as I am singing like this with him, about the girl and the let-is-zee she cooked because after we sing, come round five, Papa starts hiccupping, eyes rolling back one time, then two time, then he slouches on the sofa where the older boys sleep and by then mfana, he is snoring and snoring and scoring five bob and two shelleng from his pocket is not even a matter of skill. This one time I felt paper money in there and pulled out R2—'sTrue 'sGod! But it was too much money to get away with for carry, so I hid it and gave it to Mama and she say I did the right thing. That was the last time I ever get that much. Mama say Papa spend every-thing on cheap booze and cheaper women that one, while the Boers grow fat raping our land. Anyways that's the only thing to like about Malefa in the kitchen.

When Mama is in there I always play good little boytjie and bring a bucket of water for the sink from the outside tap and take rubbish from inside to the dump we digged under the washing line; rubbish from the pigheaded pumpkinskin Mama fight to peel, from the thin onion paper that rubs between fingers like soap and the leafy cabbage ears with holes where worms got in. My favorite is when Mama make mala le mogodu the way she make it with the crying onions, but my real favorite favorite is when she makes it story time even when she is cooking.

The story about the conniving hyena and his friend, greedy wolf, is Mama's goodest. Maybe it's because the way Mama pushes her head and chest up and down, up and down, to show

how skelem the conniving hyena is, or maybe I like it at the end
when Mama asks me again, Why is greedy wolf stupid? When
I tell Mama that Wolf is a sjupid to forget blood is thicker than
water and stupider still to trust a friend, Mama gives me a secret
smile that lets me know I am her little man and then that night I
get a real man-size meat or the whole chicken drumstick if I am
really really lucky.

It was on a night like that when the kwela-kwela started parking outside.

Me and the boys seen it first all day and I told Mama after I
looked outside the curtain at night and see magata, two of them,
and white. They not in uniform even, but nobody sits inside a
kwela—police colors barking on the outside—unless you are
one of them. I run into the kitchen where Malefa is waiting for
Mama to come back inside with the water bucket so they can
finish washing the pots and pans. Just outside the kitchen, on the
stoep, I say to Mama, Hei Mmewe, we have whites coming to
visit us! I saw them! I saw them!

Quickly, Mama push me back inside and tell me to not talk
too much if I don't know what I'm talking. But then I take her to
the window in the front room and she look through the curtain
without moving the curtain, the way she always shouts me to do
because, Do we sell fruits in this house for you to be parting the
curtains like something is for sale in here?

When she sees the kwela-kwela and the white police inside
I know enough from her look to know it's better for me to be a
good little boytjie. I walk to the kitchen where Malefa is finishing
and sit on the bench next to the sink and when I close my eyes
I see Papa coming in the door and the house is noisy again and
the stove must be burning hot the coals because it is so warm on
the inside of me and when I open my eyes again Papa is opening
another yogurt for me and asking if my favorite is vanilla or choc-

olate. I say I did not know there is chocolate yogurt. Papa laugh deep. Loud. He show me all the different yogurt I can choose. There are so many I start getting dizzy thinking which ones I will eat first and how I can eat a little bit now, then save a little, so the yogurt does not run out, so that I am eating chocolate yogurt, forever and ever. And how can I keep the icebox from melting because the house is so hot it is making my eyes heavy even when I hear loud sound, Bang! Bang! Bang! Bula! Bula! They shout, OPEN! THIS! DOOR! The door is already opening when Mama say, What?

Mama stand there with the face I see her wear when she telling Father James the only sinner she know is his god. There is a lot of noise outside. I do not understand everything too good because the police speak in deep Afrikaans and Mama answer in her English that I never hear her speaking and then there is quiet and the police is gone and I wonder is Mama maybe gone with them too? I dash out and Mama looks down. When she see me she tell me in a strange voice, Didn't I tell you to stay inside? Is something wrong with your ears? Are they just decoration? I am a little confuse because she fold me into her body after. And we stand like that in the night a long time. I hear Mama breathing.

After that the police van come and park in front of the house a lot and sometimes the policemens try and buy me with stoksweets and Coke to make friends with me but I always remember the story of the stupid wolf and conniving hyena and keep clear of the kwela-kwela. Me I pretend rats lick the Coke and stoksweets first and then they want to offer me, like I am some sjupid nje or I am greedy wolf!

Anyways, Mama has to be home always now after six o'clock and me and Malefa and Mama spend many times talking in the kitchen or behind in the back where Mama say no one can hear us.

She tell us about her family in Witbank—her sisters working

in the kitchens and brothers in the mines. She tell us a lot of stories about the crocodile and how he move his weight like a snake but a fat one that can swallow a cow. When I ask Mama if she's seen this she look at me like *I* am the one who swallowed a cow, then she ask me, What kind of crocodile are you anyway, if you don't even know bakwena powers?

Sometimes, when Mama is in the middle of the best part of the story, Malefa starts performing and Mama doesn't get to the juicy part about the girl the crocodile falls in love with, the girl who's in love with her reflection. This girl is coming to the waterhole everyday so poor kwena thinks she loves him also.

I think something is wrong inside Malefa's head these days, because her performing is too much and she seems to have some special kind of power over Mama. After she says these things to Mama—that Mama is too busy playing hide and soekmekaar, too busy sneaking into meetings to see that *The People* and *The Struggle* is nothing but dancing with danger—Mama will just be quiet and then ask her ancestors to give her strength. I shake my head at Malefa and tell her, Stop your performing! But that doesn't make things better, so I just leave the women alone and remember anyways Papa always says is something wrong with a man who needs to spend that much time with women.

Even though Mama doesn't like it, I go to the shebeen with Papa so I don't become too soft for a man. Papa always lets me sip a little taste, It's good for a man to break bread with men, Papa says, and even though I see no bread, I don't say so—it's our unspoken bind, part of our code as men. After a few rounds he always starts walking to Sfiso's and I know if I go I'll have to wait outside and hear him and Mme Zuma, so I just go back home the long way.

The last time I went out like this with Papa, I stayed out a long, long time and me and Tsepo and some other boys went to the river in Zone Six and one of the older boys showed us how to catch fish with a stick by stabbing the fish quick like a lightning bolt and striking not where the fish is standing still but two steps ahead like you are reading the fish and you know it smells fear and wants to go the other way but you are everywhere and the only way the fish can escape is dissolving in the water and what fish can do that? So I catch three little fish like this and put them inside a newspaper someone brought and the fish shine the color of stars on its belly that flops and flips funny, like when Mama tells the story I like about wolf and hyena.

I am so excited to show Mama the fish and maybe Papa will sing the song about the girl who makes bohobe with fish and we can all laugh about how funny it is and I can show them how I catch the fish with my hands like a real mokwena. I am running home all the way because I also want them to see the fish eyes. I wonder if Malefa will say the fishes have a spirit too, like dogs and cats and all the other living things witches pimp into flying familiars? But my fishes is not for witches, they are Fishy and Fishly. I have to think of a name for the other one. Maybe Fish Number Three? But that's not a good name. How would you like to be called Number Three? Just like that?

When I get home the newspaper and my pants are wet from the fish and I walk in running and don't even notice the police van is not outside and the house is quiet, so I go to the back and Malefa is sitting there and Papa is standing over her right by the dump we dug out to make a hole for Mama's rubbish. Malefa's eyes are red when she look at me and Papa say nothing. I hold out the fish to show them even though I'm not smiling anymore and I am out of breath.

Where is Mama, I ask? I have to show her something, Look at my fish! I want to show her my fish, I say. Papa look away and Malefa stare at me hard and long. She's gone, Malefa say. Mama is never coming back. I drop the fish before I know what I am doing and run inside the house to look for Mama. I find nothing.

Outside again, I force myself not to cry, to stand up like a man. But then I see Fishly and see that his eyes are dead. When I pick him up, I feel my face wet and burning with tears the color of stars.

# *Innards*

## I.

The morning the old man died, his firstborn heard him rise. Early. Said she could hear his mattress slump, fatigued. It was his heart that did him. Naledi woke before him, before the sun. Thought nothing of the laden quiet entering the house with first light as she filled the kettle, eager water hissing in a narrow stream.

The old man sat on his bed, hand to heart.

He knew so many things about the heart. He knew the shape and smell of the organ lying in a cardboard box at the slaughterhouse. The boxes went for nothing in the beginning, when he first started peddling unwanted dog meat earmarked for the dump. But then the abattoir figured if a muscled-up and capable darkie was willing to wait religiously for his butcher block dregs week after week, there was obviously some kaffir market out there worth cashing in on. Price tags latched onto the boxes. Soon, picking out the right bin without something spoiling at the bottom became Ntatemogolo's point of pride.

To pick the right heart, the old man said to look for depth in the ruby, to prize a raw intensity of color and a bright gold fat blanketing the angry muscle. He tried passing this along to his one son and double daughters. But they were repelled by his trade, wounded by its poverty. So he kept it to himself until the younger lot, the great-grandchildren especially, wanted to know what Ntatemogolo remembered. Was it true his grandfathers' grandfathers kindled rainfall for royal crops in Great Zimbabwe? That they burst rain clouds open by merely chanting their clan's praise names? Was it true Ntatemogolo could *still* coax a heart from its secret cavity and hold it in his hand so it throbbed like a newborn? Yes! Ntatemogolo would beam, Yes, it's true! You have to cradle it so its blood becomes your blood. So its arteries feel like they're pumping through *your* valves, like fresh blood is still brewing in its deepest heart of hearts.

It wasn't hard for his great-grandchildren to picture this. Until the day he died, their ntatemogolo sold innards—beastly bits of waste food no one wanted. Pork fatback and leaf lard. Sheep guts and wormy intestines. Chicken feet. Beef tongue. Bird brain and beak and vulval-pink sweetbreads believed to power unthinkable virility. He wedged his wares into a shabby bicycle basket that doubled as wandering butcher to the poorest among an already impoverished lot—old women who picked out animal fleas and stray hairs from his newspapered packages; already tar-toothed manchildren afraid of losing another limb to the mines.

Flies loved the old man, sampled everything in his path and buzzed excitedly about his balding hairline, his pungent overalls and weathered veldskoene.

He wore a daily uniform that hadn't changed in over forty years of working poverty: blue overalls, white undershirt and a brown wool balaclava for the meanest days. He owned a different overall for each weekday only after his son started working and only because that son, Modise, burned his only pair. Modise would've burned the old man's bicycle too, had it not been for Naledi.

She'd hobbled toward Modise and body slammed the full force of her limp deadweight against his narrow frame. Into the bicycle

they crashed, Modise more bewildered than beaten. Still, he paid
with sixteen stitches across his temple and a whole week's pay for
five new overalls. No one made him buy all five, but the sting of a
woman beating him in broad daylight, and a crippled one at that;
and maybe even the raging shame that burned him into destroy-
ing their father's business in the first place, it all drove Modise to
replace the one worn overall with five. The bicycle he left alone.
Besides, it still worked, and the old man was attached to it, even
if it wobbled and threatened to flatten everything in sight.

It was born rusty, Ntatemogolo's bike. Part of Modise's shame.
A bombed-out debris on wood wagon wheels and ramshackle
kind of rusty. Made in England. Probably in Coventry, back
when Europe was a Chinese factory floor and the colonies sup-
plied a hungry market for every imperial reject the mother country spawned. No one could have predicted the old man's fate back
then: death after a desperate century eking out an unyielding life,
canned grief following four stillborns and the internal inferno
of having failed the three who somehow survived. And then the
end—a dry-throated longing for a dead wife, not the two passion-
ate love affairs he'd piously coddled in the thick of his marriage.

Ntatemogolo was a child when the bike was assembled. A
herdboy who learned numbers counting cows. Five hundred and
ninety-five cattle. Sheep, goats and fowl besides. His job was tal-
lying every cow and quirk with every sunset and knowing which
was who by name. It was the beginning of the Great Wars. Ntatemogolo was a barefoot and teething shepherd back then; General
Jan Smuts a conniving double dealer busy rallying his reluctant
Boere brethren to fight, for king and country. The same king and
the same country Smuts had taken on in not one, but two bloody
Anglo-Boer wars. You can forget it, the hard-liners told him. But
Smuts was a clever Boer. He flushed out his fellow Afrikaners'
pro-German anti-Brit rebellion and sold it back to them as good

politics—after all, what's a little filth to fine fellows? Of course, in Ntatemogolo's family compound and cosmos, all that seemed far away. As if the Boers and coming wars would never touch them. As if another country, another manhood lay very close at hand— somewhere inevitable for a black shepherd boy. Rain making and black kings reigning—all that still seemed wildly possible.

But by the end of the Great Wars, Elias, as Ntatemogolo was known back then, had lost everything. His father, a menial soldier digging trenches for king and country—a glorified war mule in the South African Native Labour Corp—did not return from France. The family farm, a plump parcel on rich red earth, never stood a chance against the kleptocratic claws of Afrikaner power that soon clutched the country. The father who never returned— who fought for the British believing their promises of Native advancement, *after* the war—his absence was all the state needed to declare his land unoccupied: fallow and fertile land fit for white occupation. They gave his wife twenty-one days to cease and desist. Of course she could keep her cows, they scoffed. Five hundred and ninety-five cattle. Three hundred sheep. Forty-two lambs and ninety-eight goats. What woman could possibly manage all that? But either for native stubbornness or newfound grief, she marched those beasts across stolen farms. Somehow, Elias' mother corralled the herd to a faraway uncle who promised protection and freedom. But very soon, as soon as each hoof crossed into his kraal, that uncle counted every horned head and twin calf a new debt the young widow owed.

One hundred and six years later, the shepherd boy's heart stops. He feels its murmur slurring as he sits up, hand to chest, Naledi humming in the kitchen.

If anyone knew what signs to look for, if the line and land between his forebears and children remained unbroken, unstolen, someone would've heard the stars piercing the sky the night before. They would've begun preparations for the old man's passing the way his own mother had known to tend her affairs long before word reached that her husband would never return. They would've understood that long-tailed stars don't weep across the sky for celestial vanity. That the stars were mourning their blood.

But Ntatemogolo's children are scattered across oceans. They've long lost ties to the shallow grave dug up after Ntatemogolo's birth. To the clumps of soil, gravel and clay entombing his umbilical cord. To the earth tethering his creation to his mother's, whose birth rope is also buried in that pit, connecting every strain of blood coursing between generations . . . all the way back to that first ancestral womb.

But none of them can read the signs. Few understand how a shabby man in shabby overalls bicycling his stinky business around dusty streets could possibly be chosen. *Chosen?* Naledi would've snorted. *Chosen for what?* her mind already unraveling the dirt-poor youth it had squirreled away. None of Ntatemogolo's children could smell the iron stars smelted into their blood. And so, when Naledi limps into the room, her dead foot brushing broomlike across the floor, all she sees is her father still seated on the bed.

Strange, she thinks. He's normally dressed and worrying his wispy whiskers with that blunt razor by now. His everyday porridge thickens on the stove. She smells its sour tartness, the strong fermented scent of tieng curdling the room. The curtains are drawn. Morning light still tepid.

—Le tsugile, Ntate? Naledi asks her father.

The old man does not respond *Yes, we have risen.* Instead, he tries to heave his weight to stand. Bony elbows, bare naked and tightening chest.

Naledi rounds the bed and approaches the window. Opens the brass metal latch, breaths in brisk morning air. Still sitting, Elias—or George as he later preferred people say—feels Naledi move behind him, sees her crooked spine. Can see it in the mirror and imagine it without looking. She would've been a carbon copy of her mother, he often thinks to himself. If not for the fall. She would've become the unfettered thing he once felt pulsing in his hands when he first saw his wife: naledi—true star.

The grip in his chest tightens. Ntatemogolo releases his hand and slumps back on the bed. He doesn't mean to frighten her, but the sudden thud landing backward startles Naledi. She turns around expectedly.

She thinks she'll find something hard and heavy free-falling. A misplaced phone directory maybe or those old boots Ntatemogolo likes to store above the wardrobe. She hears hard gasps for breath instead, lungs fighting to expand, as if her father's exhalations will find more useful life outside his body. She kneels at the foot of the bed and leans in.

—Ntate? she repeats. Father?

She shakes his arm, frightened by its lightness. Her father isn't fighting but his face registers tension and his hand creeps back over his heart.

—What is it? Naledi asks.

—Ntate! Please, bathong—let me get an ambulance.

She steadies her good arm to lift herself off the floor. Ntatemogolo grabs her hand. *Stay*, his grip says. Naledi leans deeper into her functioning hand, edging closer on the bed, sitting nearer, right beside him, right on the spot where her mother's head used to rest. She tries to see what his eyes speak. He's calm. Zero panic. No last-minute flutter for flight or furious rush of words.

*I'm leaving*, he thinks maybe he should say, but decides it self-apparent. So he speaks instead to his heart, fights for calm through its sudden rage. *It's okay*, he wants to say. Naledi weeps. *Smile*, he instructs himself, but a sharp pain shoots through his left arm and he feels his heart rupture like lightning splitting its prey. He closes his eyes. Naledi's tears, her face now hovering over his, splatter stupidly onto his skin. His hand still holds hers and even though she senses danger, his grip fastens, clamping down as if the old dying man could crush her to the bone. *It's just a scare*, she thinks, reaffirming it to herself as his eyes reopen, as Ntatemogolo manages a smile. *And he is still breathing!* A soft sound stammers from the old man; a sigh.

—You're going to live, she thinks, speaking it out loud.

He smiles another smile, a narrow smile, his lips taut as his eyes flicker gently, a century's weight beating heavy against his lids. His heart, tired now but still roaring, claps a faint echo he alone can hear.

Everything fades. Dizziness floods his vision with the sudden intensity of morning light. Millions of microscopic cells that have mended his heart through love and loss, through stolen joys and naked humiliation, are now starved for oxygen. His hand slackens. The muscle's electricity flashes a final warning. Ntatemogolo opens his eyes one last time, his heart at final drumbeat. It is not Naledi's broken body and shattered face he sees, it is her mother's. His wife. Not a ghost. George does not believe in ghosts. It is her spirit. A full self-sustaining light. The electricity in his heart reroutes, grounds into earth. Naledi shuts her father's eyes and lets out a sharp wail.

# II.

### *ROSE, Rhinebeck, New York*

At this hour, the call can only be a lost drunk or ruthless creditor.
Not Naledi. *Not* asking for more money. Rose waits, expectant.
She hears her antique clock tick-tock in mock, laughing at her
insomnia. She stretches out a hand to the other side of the bed
then rolls from her tummy to her back, body naked in her ceiling
mirror.

The mirror was a gift. An installation, actually. From a student who turned out unbelievably tender-lipped for such ironclad walls. Rose let ~~her~~ them carry on about the body politic
and self-reclamation, what their art was achieving by interacting
with their bodies blah blah blah . . . plus affirmation what-what.
Rose wanted to tell her to shut the fuck up, that ~~she~~ *they* didn't
invent dykedom, that womanish men sucking cock and womanish wives husbanding women was as old as the San painted
orgies of Guruve, Zimbabwe—ancient Africans taking it in the
arse. That openly gay kings like Kabaka Mwanga II and women
bedding women—motsoalle—had long been coursing through
Rose's blood, while the white girl's people were busy roasting
~~dykes~~ witches at the stake.

Instead, Rose buried her flat nose in the girl's bulbous tissue,
the girl prattling on. She suckled. Breathed. Kneaded. The girl's
lips swelled into baby mounds of erect pink tissue, swallowing her
speech and flooding Rose's tongue with rivers of raw eggwhite.

Rose looks up. Her own deep purple cabbage-folds yawn open
like a bored preacher, staring back at her in the mirror.

She shifts, fat following form long after mindfire. Slides a
hand under her bottom-most belly roll and lifts the mass like
a veil. It flaps over her pelvic bone when Rose is standing these
days. Enough to be a nuisance, hot days especially. She thinks

about flicking the lights on, thinks about checking the time, maybe even returning to Luthuli's book. She reaches for the book. *Country of My Skull.* Hesitates. Not wanting to touch its soft skin, warm blood coursing sticky between its covers. She sits upright, thinking about her grandson, Luthuli. Edges to the end of the bed. Shoves icy feet into furry slippers—maybe that's him calling? Shuffles down the hallway and into the open living space. Fills a glass of water.

—"These young men are incredibly angry," the TV reporter says.
—"There's a lot of emotion running through these streets . . .
 George Floyd has lit a fuse. Has been a lightning rod in this
 neighborhood."

Rose recognizes the playback loop from live coverage yesterday—America burning, a blind blaze battling old bruises: George Floyd dead. Dead dead dead. Dead and gone. So far gone. She hits the Off button but cannot mute her mind. Rose thinks of fresh-slaughtered chicken. How easily chicken necks snap under the right amount of pressure, how her fisted hands twist the soft hollow cavities she likes to suck for bone marrow, how their tender strength bleats a faint pulse between larynx and trachea. A spinal injury.

And then her mind regurgitates that very last art opening, right before this whole shit show started.

—I just cannot understand why Americans cannot figure it out.

If she'd known lockdown was coming and this shitty bit of kak-talk would be her last morsel of human contact, Rose would've let this pigface piece of pinotage really fucking have it.

—Look at us, he said, thin purple veins spidery with pus under
 the surface of his see-through skin, we said goodbye to all that
 in ninety-four. Ja! After Mandela and whatnot, we ended all
 this racism rubbish. Finish 'n klaar!

That was either three pandemic months or three metamorphic

light years ago. Time—which'd always been plastic—had since collapsed. Rose had put her full glass of wine back on the counter and dug out her trench coat in the hallway closet. No goodbyes. No moment of Zen contemplating the Zwelethu Mthethwas landscaping the hallway—a trio of proud and prim shack dwellers showing off their poverty—hawking in the palatial apartment's foyer like this billionaire would throw them some bones. As she left, her fingers reached for her phone and dialed the old house number without even thinking. Because suddenly, without any warning, she just had to hear her father's voice:

—You were *working?* she'd asked him.

—*Ntate!* On a holiday?

—Because of why, Rose? her father'd teased.

—Because people are eating your holiday today? Or because these people of yours don't eat on a public holidays?

Ntatemogolo loved this joke. Loved the corny gag that kept him mounted on his bike despite his frail frame and aggressive drivers. It wasn't funny after you'd heard it the first time, but Rose and Naledi always laughed whenever he said it. Laughed at this father who found hard work so late in life; laughed at this father who'd watched them sleep hungry on countless nights, smoke rising from his full packet of cigarettes, packets that cost double one loaf of stale brown bread. The same father who drank away school fees and pissed through all the money for textbooks and uniforms and woke up too soaked for work most Mondays.

—Okay, Ntate. Rose chuckled, imagining her father run over on that stupid bike.

—Let me greet Naledi then.

She wonders now if she should call home. Hear Ntate's voice.

The television is off but the room still drones, abuzz. Rose wants to kill the static signal stuck in her mind, wants to push it back to where it came from, back to the dull numbness that allows her sleep through the nighttime and spring chicken rises when morning comes. The thing that lets her look at her grandson and feel nothing. Nothing of Freddie Gray, or George Floyd; nothing of Biko or just now-now, this new one in Alexandra, Collins Khosa. There will be no George Floyd, Breonna Taylor or Collins Khosa in Rose's Luthuli.

Rose was there at Biko's funeral. It's *his* image that's irrepressible in her mind. *His* face that superimposes itself on the countless reels of George Floyd. *His* eyes and heart and nose and mouth that also lock stiff at the rifle butt beating Collins Khosa dead. In the man's own house. In the man's own yard. In the black man's very own black country. Twenty-six years after freedom.

Biko's corpse must be so long rotten in the ground, Rose thinks. She remembers seeing his sunken eyes lying in his coffin. Neck snapped into chicken bones. Broken wing bones, clavicle, keel, rib. Broken lip too false to form any word you'd recognize as human. It was *his* face that wouldn't leave Rose, long after her daughter called yesterday, to drag up the dead. Long after Rose pretended blindness between the two police paddy wagons thrashing around, bashing black bodies.

We are the hunted, her daughter had said.

Affirm.

Rose remembers the stupid affirmations Luthuli makes her say. He frets over his gran, living alone and in the bundus despite what he calls the Boomer Remover threatening everything alive. Rose frets over her grandson, how can her brilliant Luthuli believe in fey affirmations or anything else so dumb?

—Today is a wwweally good day, she sighs, mumbling.

—Damnit! Can't say this . . . Stupid.

—*Shyyyyyyt*

She drops each word carelessly—shapeless crumbs falling out her mouth and trailing her back into bed, back between the sheets, wine bottle in hand.

—Beautiful day, she says, taking a sip of the wine.

—Mara Rose. Someone speaks. Kganthe, isn't it morning there?

Rose listens, unsure how this voice entered the house. Is it just in her head? In the room? Did she doze? How'd she pick up the phone?

—You know how many times I tried you? the voice sharpens.

—And how are you too? Rose snarls, slow, her sister's panic popping into focus.

—Listen, Rose. Naledi's voice is commanding.

Rose wants to snap.

—Rose! Are you sitting?

—*Naleeedi!* Rose slurs. Are you drinking?

*Really, Naledi!* Rose thinks, now sitting up in bed with her brow furrowed, wine bottle empty and back against the headboard:

—What's this?

She feels a thick fog reach across the ocean and through the phone line. As soon as Naledi suggests sitting, Rose feels this fog shift the weight of the room. And knows.

—When did it happen? she asks Naledi. Even. Removed.

Naledi recounts her morning. Rose imagines their father as her sister speaks. Sees him in that bare-arsed room, sees him sitting at the edge of his bed, his hand growing heavy on his chest like Naledi keeps repeating, pictures it slackening onto the mattress. Onto their mother's side. The clean side, which would've been leveled like a sand dune that morning. Iron flat since the day Naledi called with the same news about Mma. About Ntate, waking next to his wife's cold and sleeping body. Eighteen months, three weeks, six days and eleven hours ago. Naledi saying, Mma's face was frozen to frost. That her cold hands and placid face held something pure. Remembers how, afterward, after Mma's burial and official mourning period passed, how she'd felt her father's eyes searching for his dead wife's. Searching like she'd be on the other side of an opening door—his missing sock in hand or a sharp word for his sloth, a knowing look on her face.

Had Mma been there this morning, Rose thinks, had her impressive mass of skin, dimpled tallow and royal bones risen up beside Ntate, he would've told her about his heart. He would've waited until Mma was dressed and near the door with her chamber pot and complained in a matter-of-fact voice so she'd understand: *This is different.*

Rose sees her in the doorframe. A tall woman, their Mma. Even in old age. A tall dark woman with thin lips stretching wide across her face. An extravagant serving of skin in that strange empty space where mouths rise to meet noses. And if their father had complained about his heart, Rose can see the line and curve of the smile Mma would've offered him. The private one. The one Rose and her siblings pretended not to know about. The one that married Mma to Ntate more than any officiant or lobola slaughtered for Mma, more than any son she ever bore him.

But of course, their mother is long in the ground. Rose has kept count. Eighteen months, three weeks, six days and eleven hours. She wonders, almost out loud to Naledi, if Mma had any happiness seeing the old man suffer this morning. Even if only briefly, like a false start. Because aren't our dead a silent witness? Because hadn't *she* suffered? All those years and years of unspoken unsayables. *You've never been married,* Mma would say. Not as a put-down, the way she said it. More a plain statement of fact. Like the sun is a violent star and yet it also sustains you.

# III.

### *KENEILWE, Adams Morgan, D.C.*

—Ntate's dead. Rose cuts straight to the bone. Not knowing how else to say the thing, how to slice it into tiny pieces.

—Kene, she tries again.

—The deceased . . . George. Your grandfather . . . Ntatemogolo is gone.

Keneilwe hears her mother breathing steadily into the phone. She fights down the tight knot fastening in her throat.

—Ntatemogolo? she begs.

Her mother does not respond, does not say the kind of things Keneilwe will soon say to her own son, putting his loss before hers. Rose's way, Keneilwe thinks, feeling buried barbs resurface between them.

—I should've known. Keneilwe mouths, muttering.

Speaking more to herself than to her mother, ignoring the finality of Rose's pronouncement:

*Dead.* Gone. Ntatemogolo's dead.

—Wow! Keneilwe sighs.

—But he sounded so strong . . . I just called him.

She feels a strange wave of depletion. Like someone came from behind and stole something inviolable. Her shadow, maybe. Or breathing.

—Do you know I saw him in a tree? she hears herself saying.

—Keneilwe? her mother calls out, brittle concern seeping into her voice.

—What're you saying, Kene?

But Keneilwe is gone, her concentration on a young tree she saw on a day she spoke with her grandfather. An autumn tree.

On a tiny street in Chinatown. A lone sapling blooming in mid-November. Before Miss Rona. Its tight fists of green buds shooting springtime blossoms. She'd stopped and stared, cocooned in one of those black sleeping bags she hates about America. Stopped to look up from the middle of the street and frown. The tree just plain ignored all the others around it, busy undressing, busy getting ready for snow and stoic stillness and winter sleep. What's going on in *those* roots? she remembers thinking.

Because trees are funny. Very deep thinkers. Raw data travels up their trunks. Up thick fibers and veins, carrying water and food. Knowledge of ancient rain patterns, invasive neighbors and coming disease—it's all passed between the root and its shoot like an underground railroad. A webbed brain that switches on at first frost or late snow or a bad storm threatening to butcher creaking bark.

There must've been a billion counts of microscopic warnings and cellular intelligence that somehow failed to enter the bloodstream of that lone blooming tree.

Or maybe it knew, Keneilwe thinks, considering Ntatemogolo's one hundred and six years of winter. How he loved and kept loving despite his harsh climate. Rose's patience thins on the line, listening to silence.

Maybe that tree bloomed in spite of a damned truth.

# VI.

## *HEARTH, Soweto*

It is many Sundays ago. Mma still confined to bloody flesh and brittle bones.

She stands in the kitchen, chamber pot in hand, nightgown long and thin under an unbelted secondhand robe Rose foisted on her one Mother's Day. Her husband—a reedy man whose yeasty breath has fouled her waking hours for seventy-one years—stirs in the next room. She opens the kitchen cabinet, fishes out her toothbrush and dry toothpaste and puts them on the counter. Squeezes the tube till a thin-spined, neon-color worm wriggles onto worn bristles. Brush in mouth and chamber pot sloshing with warm urine, Mma heads outside to the tap and toilet.

Later, midmorning and up the road, Ntatemogolo sits sober as a hymn. A junior pastor warms up the congregation, the head preacher looking on with what he hopes seems divine seniority but is in fact naked rivalry. The flock pretends not to notice. For weeks, the clergical understudies have been calling for God's children to leave Egypt and its wicked Pharoah, their boss snidely responding with laden text about "slaves obeying earthly masters" and "sons honoring fathers."

Ntatemogolo listens, dozing at the sonorous competition and letting out a soft snore.

Back in the kitchen, Mma is surrounded by her own flock.

—And you two? Mma preaches.

—Vele, you're going to just sit there staring at me? Just like that?

She shoots Rose, Naledi, Keneilwe, her grands, and great-grands a sharp look:

—What? You've all turned into men? Should I bring you cold beers?

Naledi and Rose rise, but Mma throws both hands on her hips and marching orders this way and that:

—Grab a knife!

—Peel the pumpkin!

—Where's the cabbage?

—Kgante keng? Did I raise a bunch of useless swines or what?

The whole kitchen springs into motion—knives peeling, hands scrubbing, bodies sweeping and the sweet smell of salty caramel rising from the stove as Keneilwe slow-cooks onions in Rajah's colonial-India curry.

Mma's legs splay wide. Her thighs and hips and buttocks spread out, like wide ostrich wings trapped under the small kitchen table. Naledi, who sits opposite, watches Mma dribble her tea; sees her pour the frothy milk from cup to saucer, then lean her chin forward to suck slow sips off the saucer.

—Too hot, Mma says, tutting at the vacuum sound her spit makes to slurp the tea.

The whole time, watching Mma, Naledi rolls a big, thick-skinned squash toward her limp arm and uses her stump's smooth deadness to hold down the bumpy squash. She grabs a fat butcher blade in her good hand. And pretends not to notice the brown rivulet snaking down her mother's chin, past Mma's neckline and onto her chest. A small dark pool clouds Mma's dress where the tea drops gather.

—Your mother! Naledi bellows, gesturing to her niece, Keneilwe, who is standing at the stove, back facing the room. Keneilwe turns around at this, at the thick syrup coating her auntie's laugh.

—Your mother; that Rose! Let me tell you. Before all this gay nonsense, she lusted after Phelonious Grootboom like a sewer sloth fighting for freak licks from a frog!

Naledi chuckles, remembering Rose from before-before.

—Naledi! Mma cuts in, not needing another word.

Not even looking up from her saucer slurps to stare Naledi down. The youngest in the room, Mma's great-granddaughter, steals a quick glance at her Mmamogolo Rose and decides from Rose's face that a small chuckle is safe.

—Anyways. Naledi continues, undeterred.

—Nobody had money like that Phelonious back then. Maybe that's why your mother liked him? Kere diDollar, baby!

Naledi gestures with her good hand, shaking the knife like a flag. And grins.

—Rose, she says.

—Remember how he had all of Diepkloof's only phone? Remember how he refused to let anyone touch it?

Naledi waves a moon-shaped squash peel in the air to make her point, telling her Johnny-come-lately nieces what they'd never understand. The pumpkin's dark skin glistens like wet moss. And its yellow insides, now hollowed out, look like tufts of bad hair dangling from a comb.

—His was the only telephone from Baragwanath to Black Chain. From Zone Six and a-a-a-all the way to those mine dumps ko Zone Four!

—You know those dumps are radioactive, right? Keneilwe asks no one in particular.

—Ja. Keneilwe continues, responding to her own question:

—I read it in the *Guardian*. Bare uranium. Bare, that's why those klein koppies are that weird pus color. That yellow fever color.

—He Banna! Naledi belts, her patchwork beard seemingly growing longer with her disbelief.

—Hai suka man, wena Keneilwe! Naledi clicks her tongue.

—All these years we've lived here in peace and now all of a sudden

some white man *know-all* ko boLondon who's never even been
to Soweto tells you we have radio action and you go around
believing him? And now you wanna go around telling *me* that
we're nogmal full of yellow fever? What radio action? Where
did you hear this? And since when do bourgie babes like you
know the first one plus one about yellow fever?

The kitchen cackles. Everyone giggling, each one of these
women not wanting to admit to the cancer-rich uranium lurking
in those mine dumps. Laughing hard to bury-dead the regular
reports of trashed bodies and corrective gang rapes swallowed by
that same sallow Soweto soil.

—Naledi! Rose cuts through the high-pitched gaggle.

—I don't know why you're digging up a dead man. You know
　Abuti Phelo left the same year as Modise? Right after Luthuli
　came. What was that, Kene? Rose asks her daughter, as if she
　could ever forget Luthuli's birth year.

—Hmmmn! Naledi huffs.

—That Phelonious bastard's mother should've maimed him when
　she had the chance—before he was even born!

—He Bathong! Naledi! O jeleng? How can you say that? Rose
　asks, glaring at her sister.

—And *why* would you say that? Who deserves death?

—That dog Phelonious, Naledi fires back, quick. That Phelonious
　Grootboom dirty snake in the grass!

—Poh! she then spits, raising her ugly stump to her mouth and
　scrunching her face, as if the dry spit were in fact thick and
　wet with phlegm.

A silence stiffens whatever laugh was still limbering around
the kitchen on shaky legs. Mma clears her throat but does not
speak. Keneilwe, now at the sink with hands sogged in green
Sunlight soapsuds, wades into the tension:

—All *I* remember, she begins, is that one time we were playing at Caretaker's. You remember mos, Mamogolo Naledi? she asks her aunt.

—You remember how we were playing at Caretaker's and Zungu got into that stupid fight and Abuti Phelo said his phone wasn't for little kaffirtjies when we asked, *Can we please call an ambulance?* And then Zungu bled to death?

—And how was that Phelo's fault? Rose snaps at her daughter.

—I mean. You do realize the Boers didn't send baboons ambulances, *don't you?*

Mma sucks her teeth and looks down at her tea. There's nothing left but a faint ring round the rim of her cup. She looks around and sees her husband's features spread evenly across the room. *His* proud nose stiffening Keneilwe's face. *His* gathered brow and tight face claiming Naledi's narrowed eyes and indignant concern.

—Like apartheid was Abuti Phelo's fault! Rose smacks her lips.

Her father's cheek, that one, Mma continues to herself.

—I'm telling you, Rose! Naledi says, standing from the table, stirring salt into the pot.

—They're now saying your "Abuti" Phelo was working for Special Branch ke go botse! A payrolled informer, Rose. Sies, man! This bloody ANC, amasela nje.

Naledi spits another dry curse over her shoulder, saying nothing of their brother, Modise, and the long shadow his history casts.

—iMpimpi! Naledi repeats. Him and that cheap Colored in the papers last week, calling himself a doctor. Sies, man! Dr. P-h-Demagogues these ANC people.

—Yes! Keneilwe blurts out, excited.

—I read that story too! Dr. Basters! In the *Sunday Times*. A fake Dr. PhD who was once a known askari. And the ANC made him a minister. Can you imagine?

And then Keneilwe tries to steady the steer, to channel the brewing thunder and lightning someplace without storms:

—Do you know they named a primary school after him? Dr. Basters, I mean. In Lady Grey? Eastern Cape? Dr. Basters Primary School. What do they tell those children now? We'll teach you how to fake your PhD? And who thinks to name a place of learning Bastard Primary?

The lightning catches fresh electricity, again riding laughter, again flashing sparks throughout the warm and crowded kitchen.

In church, Ntatemogolo dozes. Lightly. The pastor thunders, pretending his geriatric flock an army of ravenous believers. He preaches in dictionary English, thumping the Bible for confirmation and sweeping his brow for fervor. One of his warring juniors interprets, skipping entire paragraphs and inconvenient passages, delivering his droll Sepedi translation in a distant and disapproving manner.

Ntatemogolo—who once worked at Moretsele's on Pritchard Street, who regularly served and overheard deep intellectual spars between the young lawyers Mandela and Tambo and their educated ilk—knows enough big English to recognize pretentious slapdashery when he hears it. He shakes off his sleep and stands up to leave.

In the kitchen, his womenfolk have stretched out into Sunday afternoon. Luthuli and his male cousins have also arrived, buying everyone brightly colored sugar drinks and the obligatory Coca-Cola. Fresh chicken pieces simmer on the two-plate, their warm spices suffocating the cramped three rooms. Mma insisted on cooking the bird herself, meaning they'll soon be suffering through overcooked mush that won't strain her husband's jaw.

—So, Mma, Luthuli asks his grandmother's mother, where's Ntatemogolo?

—Ha! Naledi scoffs, responding as if asked, and still guzzling down her fizzy drink.

—Wena Luthuli, you know where he is! Naledi says.

—Phela ke weekend. Where else do you think your Ntatemogolo is?

—Praying for Zuma! Keneilwe butts in, winking at her son.

—Well then, Rose throws an arm round Luthuli's shoulder, in *that* case! He'll be praying till Kingdom come!

Mma laughs with all her blood, standing time still on her small claim of earth. She belts out a hoot, the moment's simple sweetness stretching out like ugly belly skin making room for new life.

—Eish! Naledi gesticulates with her hands, mara these politicians. Remember when JZ said he'd shit all over us till Jesus returns?

—And who believed him? Mma asks between whimpered breath, wiping off her laughing tears.

—*You!* an unsteady voice growls.

Mma turns to face the voice, chest chuckle still heaving.

—You! the voice grows louder:

—You sheep who vote for the ANC . . . They shear your brains, those people! It doesn't matter their scandals, shem . . . Marikana! Nkandla! Guptagate! When it comes time to voting, you people gonna vote ANC!

It's Ntatemogolo shouting, suddenly at the door. Swaying.

—Ja! He doubles down, finger wagging at a laughing Mma.

*Ntatemogolo!* Everyone greets him, making room for the old man and making a fuss. Le tsugile? they ask him, How did you rise? Luthuli gets up, his great-grandfather wobbling into his now empty seat, no balance in his missteps to sit down.

—Ntate is right, Rose agrees, returning to an earlier argument.

—Of course the Boers stole! Their whole race invented thieving!

But this kak-cake you guys call a demo-kleptocrat? We didn't petrol bomb this country just for some black rapists to take over the white ones.

—So you want to take us back? Naledi asks her sister. Vote *in* that DA's Darkie Aversion party and bring back their favorite bioscope, *Apartheid: The Sequel*?

—N e b b b e r! Ntatemogolo slurs, the word falling from his mouth like a Slinky toy. His wife and children turn to look at him, to listen, whatever he has to say. He burps instead, a loud foul sound that hiccups and agitates Mma.

—Go sleep, then! she snaps, her husband now tottering, getting up from the bench.

Naledi, closest to the little bench, pretends she hears nothing, smells nothing, even as Rose tenses up. Mma shakes her head and sucks her teeth. Each woman playing her role in an old routine.

—What's that? A great-grand asks, scrunching her face.

Another giggles uncomfortably, till Keneilwe slaps her bare thigh.

—Ntatemogolo? Luthuli startles, grabbing his elder's sleeve, balancing his lurch, walking them both.

—He just needs fresh air, Naledi lies.

Luthuli leads Ntatemogolo out the door, to the back rooms outside. The women look away from each other, from the husband, father and grandfather shuffling past them like an outed clown, a wet butterfly bleeding patiently through his pants. Keneilwe finally finds a dry cloth inside the night bucket under the sink, to sop up the piss.

Naledi and Mma stare blankly, an unmoved audience at a stiff and predictable concert—the emperor once again laying everything bare.

Outside, Ntatemogolo sings. Loud. Loud enough to hear him inside, some bent-up tune that has Luthuli laughing, adding a mumbled hook all his own.

—Jesus! Rose says, spitting at the puddle.

—Can't believe this filthy shit. She huffs. After all these years!
How's that man *still* a drunk?

—A drun*k*? Mma slaps an extra consonant around the *k*.

—The hell you mean, *a drunk*?

—I mean your husband is an alcoholic, Mma. Rose is louder than
she intends.

—Like a sewer rat. A wreck—your man ke sebotho. Have you
ever met a bottle he won't drain?

A worn discomfort cools the room.

—Ntatemogolo isn't a drunk, Keneilwe says, softly. Shamefully.

—He only drinks on the weekend. And it's Sunday, Mma, Kene
offers. Everyone deserves a little weekend special.

Rose gets up to leave. Not saying, Those little weekend spe-
cials cost us a five room home with indoor plumbing. Not saying, We were evicted like thieves because Ntate drank the rent
away. Not saying anything about all the times Ntate passed out,
all the countless times Mma or Naledi or Rose herself washed out
his soiled pants. Not even mentioning Naledi's broken spine, the
fault line where all the family's earthquakes started. How Ntate
robbed his firstborn of everything, even her unborn babies.

—Your father's been through a lot, Mma says, her voice quiet as
Rose brushes past.

—And what, Mma? Rose demands.

—You haven't?

# V.

## *GENESIS*

After Mma died, the crowded kitchen felt too large and unsettled for Naledi, who cooked only on Sundays anyways and only freezer-friendly food. And Ntatemogolo didn't eat. Only baby-soft pap with inkomasi sometimes or beef chotlo other times. But Naledi never worried.

Ntatemogolo's pockets were littered with little bags of chewed meat—congealed jelly babies that looked like witchcrafted people made of pap handfuls and wors. She'd fish out the food alongside small change and old receipts with all the ink smudged off. Some paper money every now and then.

Naledi only wondered if her father still paid for everything on credit, or if the shebeen queen had fleeced him for so much and for so long that she felt obliged to feed the old man something sturdy with his midday beers.

After emptying each pocket and soaking his overalls in warm water—her good hand beating cloth against the outdoor washboard—Naledi would hang her father's whole wardrobe across the line. Five overalls if it wasn't a weekday. Three pairs of socks and a few mismatched couplings; then his one good pair of pants and the four shirts he alternated on Sundays.

Looking at the clothes, you'd never know Ntatemogolo was once a dandy. You'd never imagine the young man in his handsome fedora and brand new name—all bits of a careful costume worn for Johannesburg, all carving distance from that long-ago shepherd boy.

Because George E. Sebotse arrived in Gauteng already imagining himself fast and slick and city-schooled. A real klever. A backwater Pedi whose tongue couldn't unfasten fast enough to force out the city's lingua franca, isiZulu. A freshly circumcised

initiate who faltered knifing disrespectful loud mouths, but glee-
fully teased every other Jimmy Come to Jo'Bek. He bought himself a lockback Okapi and hugged it to his waist. He drawled
his walk and added a light dap dance to his step. He studied
Sophiatown's American and Gestapo gangs, blending in with
that crowd.

And he might as well have done all this upon arrival, on his
very first day in Johannesburg. So cocksure and still tall in himself. Unbelieving of the truth that spread like a plague all around
him—the black bodies collapsing underground while shoveling
shale and shifting sand. Or the ones who survived this golden
gut but climbed out with blackened lungs and hard-boiled brains.

George could not see any of this, arriving in Johannesburg,
standing at the bus stop— corner Biccard and De Korte. All
he saw were the impressive triangular post office and Victorian
storefronts, the whitewashed churches and private homes painted
with more ornate detail than any three-tiered wedding cake.

He couldn't yet see Johannesburg for the filthy whore she
really was—a scoundrel rat fink who'd porn her own mother's
birth canal to the highest bidder. He couldn't yet tell the pretty
houses from the drinking holes stuffed with pretty young things
white men fetched from the East End, from Parisian perfumer-
ies and maisons closes, and from Russian gangsters running the
loose streets of Lithuania. George could barely name the French-
fontein bars and back-alley shebeens where these girls served up
twin titties a ha'penny—color bar be damned.

He waited for his bag on the edge of the road. The air was
hot and stiff. Still. Sweating. Cars and cyclists speeding without pause. His suitcase was on the bus roof. Next to bicycles and
clothing bundles wrapped in torn sheets. By shiny tin kettles and
zinc tin tubs clinking and clapping, chafing against tatty rope
tying everything together. The roof was overstuffed, bursting.

With live chickens even. Everything on top, helter-skelter. As though the bus wore a battered crown weighing it down.

The driver climbed the bus' rear and stood on its spine. Dumped people's things overboard, loosely, absently, without a single care. Like rubbish. He panted. A porky man, the bus driver. Quickly growing breathless and sweaty. Completely disinterested in the passengers and their things, in the stray paw-paws and avocados running free from mishandled bags, running away from the bus driver, bouncing on the roof and landing in the street, splattering into dust.

George's bag was yellow or green or some other color that once promised prosperity. Light. His whole world between its ribs. Wanting. Next to the heft and worldliness the other bags carried, George's looked emaciated. Which may explain why George exploded when the driver tossed it without any thought and the sick little thing split into two.

All its insides spilling out, gushing and rushing like desperate diarrhea the slim bag could no longer hold. George's meager world splayed itself to Johannesburg: his wedding blanket and tobacco pipe, his hair comb with metal teeth. A change of shoes and extra pair of pants. All a confused pile flying around.

George, new to the city and with everything to prove, took the mishap as his first test of manhood. Before the bus driver stepped down the last rung in the rear ladder, George was in his face, fire in his fists and the devil on his tongue.

—You bloody bastard! he yelled, drawing a crowd.

—You savage piece of shit! Whose things you think you're throwing like that?

The driver, still sweating under the weight of all those bags, still calm and double George's paltry size, wiped his brow with a deft backhand and tried to swat away this fly. And that must've been the trigger. The arrogant dismissiveness, the confident conclusion of that move. George leapt toward the bus driver with everything he had. Threw punches and kicks and every muscle with flex. The crowd shouted excitedly. Other passengers and random pedestrians stopped going about their business to stop and to stare, arms folded or standing akimbo, a few people cheering.

The bus driver was in the dust, arms blocking blows like a fortress; his demeanor strangely calm. He was not fighting George, he was biding time. If George were not a country bumpkin, were he not so freshly minted and already swelling with Jozzie's false and hollow pride, he would've smelled something strange in the blood drawn from the driver's nose. He would've noticed that the fat man held his nose against the rush of red without alarm. He would've heard him grunt and understood such smug content couldn't come from a man being badly beaten.

By the time the bus driver's goons surrounded George, seemingly appearing out of nowhere, Jo'Bek had darkened herself and disappeared the cheering crowd. The men dragged George away from the road, away from oncoming traffic and any threat of authority. They pummeled him into a tattered tire. His lungs coughed blood and his heart shouted, STOP.

Years later, he'd know from this moment exactly what his little girl felt lying in a broken puddle herself, wondering, *Is* this *how it ends?*

In that future, George returns to their rented shack and hangs up his hat. On a day he was fired. For forgetting himself. Calling his employer's seven-year old Matilda. Opening the car door too late for *Miss* Matilda. Making *Miss* Matilda walk without stepping aside to let *Miss* Matilda pass.

He sways as he lifts his firstborn, but still manages to look strong to his wife. Strong and beautiful—the way things easily broken beckon.

He hoists Naledi up. His true star without trace of night. Up she goes and down again, caught in his outstretched arms. She laughs and laughs, a sound that will haunt him for seventy-seven years to come. A full-throttle and trusting sound. He throws her up, higher and higher, like a boomerang comet ricocheting to earth. Confident of his quick reflex and flexed muscles—certain he only had three shots and two beers, not six shots and nine beers—he smiles.

And his smile, a wide grin plastered on his face like plastic blackness, is the very first thing that drops. It sags 'round his knees before thudding hard against the dirt floor; Naledi following, hatching into a chirpless chicklet beside George's stupefied grin. She looks small, baby Naledi. So small. A tiny breathless bird flattened on its back. Face up. Beak shut. She lies there like he lay, unresponsive and unbelieving, floating between conscious bewilderment and the dark forest of night.

# VI.

## *MODISE, Friedrichshain, Berlin*

Answering his sister, Modise says yes, but knows he means no.

—I will come, he says.

He doesn't ask, *How?* With all of Europe now shoveled under China's shit? With half the living world dead or freshly dying?

He digs his bare hands into cool morning earth, back bent and face tight; uproots a thorny weed with sharp red hairs that choke around the throat of his young lilac bush.

*Ntate is dead*, Modise repeats to himself, convincing himself. My father is dead.

He stands in the garden and feels his mind loosen. The birds are too loud. The gnats too many, too sticky to his skin. His thoughts grow wild, slow and soft—like his head is emptying itself—raw lava returning to mud.

He hears Naledi say Ntate's grip was ironclad. Strong. That his whole body sweated after, soaked the bedsheets wet as yellowed piss. That part jolts Modise's mind back into the bloody phone line. Gets his goat. Naledi and her tongue. Does she have to shit scheisse every time she opens that mouth? Even at Ntate's death?

Modise drops to the ground. His shins sink in, soft hair clutching the smallest grains of his store-bought loam. It does not smell like soil. It's fuller and richer, sweeter too. As if someone imagined a recipe for how to make good earth but lacked all the grayness of death, that fattens living soil.

He listens. Lets his sister drone on in morbid detail. Because the pandemic did things to people. Fucked with their faculties. Even him. That's why, when the global house arrest first started, he'd gone back to the most unfuckablewith element: basic math. Hard numbers.

You can't fuck with the square root of sixty-four. Eight is two by four in every language. Bet. And if you add two special numbers, the sum of their parts squared is the same as those two special numbers standing next to each other, skin to skin:

$$494 + 209 = 703$$
$$703^2 = 494{,}209$$
$$8 + 1 = 9$$
$$9^2 = 81$$

Get a prime factorization of $10^n - 1$ and your ass lands with one of those Kaprekar numbers, no matter what. There you are, swimming in the soft brown matter of Dattatreya Ramchandra Kaprekar, a lowly Indian school teacher nobody minded till a famous white American baptized his numbers.

Modise discovered all this alongside the simple satisfaction of 1,729. Back when shit really hit the fan. Back when Suliman first disappeared and Modise's brain broke under detention without trial. Even in a black hole, he discovered, 1,729 remains the smallest number you can express as the sum of two different cubes in two different ways:

$$10^3 + 9^3 = 1{,}729$$
$$12^3 + 1^3 = 1{,}729$$

Hardy-Ramanujan's number.

One thousand seven hundred and twenty-nine made sense to him even then, inside the farthest reaches of that stellar black hole, where urinating on himself mid-sentence seemed a perfectly good response, where sentences tore apart as soon as you opened your mouth, so that their subatomic parts drooled into a dense and inarticulate murmur. 1,729 saved Modise when nothing else could.

And maybe even before that. When he was just a snotball starting to smell himself. When Ntate's servile nakedness humiliated him, didn't it, Modise? Ntate's total lack of manhood, even as police paraded it like that; your father's blue-black genitals swinging like frenzied rattle balls ringing in the street.

Modise started counting then. All the policemen in the yard. One. Two. Three. All the fathers and grandfathers and uncles and brothers shaken like loose litter from their houses, the few police moving door to door along a pitch-dark street. Twenty-five men on a busy night. Twelve or six when things were quiet. A dozen grown-ass men to only three enemies. A dozen to twenty-five grown men who couldn't protect you, Modise, who answered to some other man calling them *Boy*.

You disavowed Ntate then, didn't you, Modise? And hated everything about him. Did the math on *that* ratio and decided your father a coward.

Modise says the number out loud.

—One thousand seven hundred and twenty-nine: one, seven, two, nine.

—Modise? Naledi asks.

He ignores his sister. Repeats the number because it soothes him. Because isn't this how you claw yourself out of a black hole? Back into spacetime? Modise kept track of the losses in bare bones and numbers.

Standing naked at Number Four. Arse clenched into a fist. He counted ninety-seven black bodies around him. Ninety-eight arrested men stripped of everything and snaking in the line ahead. One old man made to wriggle like a maggot, made to dance—to throw his shriveled testicles to the wind—till the warden was satisfied at the sight of this elder thrusting his cheeks into a wide cleft part. You were what? Sixteen? Seventeen? You'd already spent 139,128.036 hours on earth.

Number two in line, up ahead by the district surgeon, wagged his tongue and clucked his arms. Submitted to examination like spoiled butcher meat. You counted all the instruments on the doctor's table. Figured there were at least nine sharp pieces on that wooden table—scalpel, pinwheel, scissors—nine things to arm ninety-eight naked men waiting like sheep to be processed by seven guards plus one prison surgeon.

You hated your father, didn't you, Modise? Battered. Beaten. Left with nothing but his stupid pride. A pride that smelled worse than his bicycle offal shit, a pride that couldn't protect you.

And you hated yourself. Hated everything you'd become over the years, to survive. The prisoner who imprisoned all his comrades. The snitch and askari, impimpi—who sang and sang and sang to save his own hide.

We survived, Modise thinks. Him a whole century. Me—I survived myself.

Enough surviving for people to think it was nothing. For the state to claim it all over. Even in Berlin. Where people say it's the Jews and the Gypsies, *they* did all the suffering. Maybe a few Tutsis. And now these Ukrainians. What you survived, what you *still* survive, it's Oppression Olympics bringing any of it up.

My father is dead, Modise thinks.

—Ntate is dead. That's what Naledi said.

They bury him the next week. Lower him in the ground. Ntate-mogolo's only son will not come home; Modise will not throw fresh earth over his father's flesh. He will pace this Friedrichshain house, the sun sitting up. Drown in drink. And he will cry. After. Long after the burial. After the grave is full. After everything the young shepherd boy could've been. After Ntate's body burnishes clean to the bone, after his wormy innards butcher him into feast and fattening, feed for the soil.

# VII.

## *LUTHULI, Bed-Stuy, Brooklyn*

In the dream, my great-grandfather enters the room.

First, I hear his bicycle wheels brake and then *feel* him. Smell his innards—dead meat sunning in the basket. Spoiling. Swarming with flies.

Second, I follow him

In

To their room. My great-grandmother, Mma, is on all fours. Naked on the ground. Eyes far, jaw set. A piercing belly full. I see Ntatemogolo lower his length to the ground. I see his arms circle Mma's full girth, follow his legs webbing around hers like a spider.

Mma leans her spine against his chest. Loud pounding sound—through skin and spine I hear their twin hearts. She pushes and pushes. *Push*—Ntatemogolo coaxes from behind—till a little head crowns. Blue, then purple. Hush. A hush. No sound. Limp strands of father mother blood covered in caul.

In this dream, Ntatemogolo keels.

Mom's call comes a few hours later. I do not share this strange dream. Do not ask, why would Mma visit to show me her stillborn? I forget my great-grandfather's words, *Our star was born long-tailed.* Was the fetus his star, mourning silently through the sky?

—Luthuli, Mom says.

—Ntatemogolo has passed.

—The old man is gone.

# 7678B
# Chris Hani Road

*We knew 7678B had taken up with the devil. Mara,* jirrre*!* Even baloi ba tshiritshiri couldn't be blamed for the kind of bad-blooded bedevilment that came over Boytjie and Barnabas.

There were whispers Makhadze started the stink. That after the old bat got 7678B's first family running numbers, the house became a seedbed for every nasty knave spirit rejected by the ancestors. But that was rubbish. Makhadze was long in the ground—dead and gone when the whole shitstorm started. And anyways. People who know these things, people who knew Boytjie and Barnabas from before 7678B, they say the twins were born in battle. They say a live snake poisoned them in the womb, that it weaned the pair off their mothermilk and cut them from her cord.

Whatever it was, there was never a more deadly war.

Some even believe Boytjie *gave* her brother the sickness. Of course, you can never speak such a thing out loud. And yet . . . everyone—including people who profited from Ousie Boytjie's spaza bank—everybody sensed something dark and sinister the real source of Boytjie's money. And that her fortune was yoked to her brother's stinky luck the way a thorny headed tapeworm chains itself to now-now rotting intestines.

Knowing all this, it really shouldn't have come as a surprise, seeing Tom's old house blazing down as it finally did—fighting to bury Ousie Boytjie alive. *And yet!* How we circled that house—excited hyenas surrounding a carcass. How we let 7678B reel us in, outfox us all—so long before the old cinderblock's big burn even.

To think of it now, that house was *always* burning. A slow smolder stewing, just like Bra Barney's sickness. And of course, township gossips—boshwashi, they say the wickedness caught even *before* Barney's sickness, that it was lit by Tom and Ethel Fakude's black luck—a young and healthy husband, so sudden kaput. Out of nowhere—just dead and gone. Full stop. And then his mourning widow flushed out like shit down a toilet. People say 7678B was never the same.

But death is nothing new. The Fakudes were far from the first. Full flocks of believers and vagabonds have been known to perish from parishes since the arrival of Boers. Entire bloodlines erased and generations of burial grounds and grain and grassland exhumed from yielding earth. There was really nothing special about 7678B's evictions—at least three comma five million darkies were forcibly removed, long before the Fakudes. Tom and Ethel had no worse luck than the rest of us.

*And yet.* 7678B stood empty so long, it became a dumping ground.

Following Ethel's exit—when we were still under boot of the Boers and the Brits, hangmen who confiscated our country—7678B stood rancid, spoiling. Spider mites bludgeoned the hydrangeas. Tom's fecund rosebush floundered, eaten by a sallow rust the way a small flame singes paper to gray ash. And the climbing morning glory Tom coaxed into a lush shawl blanketing 7678B's front fence shot up, untamed, overwhelming the wire wall. Rotten apricots splattered their worm-riddled flesh and wild weeds smothered the browning grass. 7678B was infested. The ripe raw smell of overgrown things strangling its veins.

Then along came Barnabas. Even before he moved in, everybody knew Barnabas. He was the Phuzekhemisi-blasting uncle who embarrassed you, the one who came from the armpit depths of kwaZulu Natal's rolling hills, earlobes dangling to shoulders like loose genitals. He was the Venda husband who spoke too loud and ate mounds of maize meal open-mouthed, soft chewed pap clumps falling from his maw. He was the Malawian migrant who dressed even louder than his homeland's pink flamingos and gray crowned cranes put together, splashing his little mine-money on open-toe mbatatas and blinding neon button-downs. When we laughed at him, it wasn't in secret or hiding our disdain. We were laughing at our own uselessness and shame: our naked poverty and oily submission.

Because Barnabas was back-asswards country. A real Johnny-come-lately who wore his ignorance like a badge shouting something sullying about our blackness.

How Bra Barney, as Barnabas came to be known, landed 7678B was through a washed-out, old-timey thug named Ephraim.

Bra E was a smallscore Sophiatown tsotsi who remade himself in Soweto as the people's pundit. His craft was petty dealings and bribes. He could make a robbery case disappear for around five klipper. That easily doubled if you'd been stupid enough to shake down a white household without first recruiting the help. For a long time, there was a rumor Bra Ephraim was peddling raw diamonds from his native Maseru and siphoning fat profits into arms for the struggle. But there were a lot of problems with that rumor.

For one, Bra E lived in his mother's original, standard-issue, government grade GG house. Just like 7678B. No improvement whatsoever. And number two, Bra E got none of the ANC's Ransack & Development Ponzi scheme when they eventually swept into power.

Even still, before that liberation gravy train, before its eager caesars saw fit to rename Old Potchefstroom Road for Chris Hani, anything requiring buttering the Boers—Bra E was your man. *Anything*—as long it wasn't justice.

How Barney fell in with Bra E—that we really don't know. But for sure Bra Ephraim was how Barnabas scored 7678B. And a lot of things were strange with this arrangement. Barney lived alone.

Nobody lived alone, not back then. Much less a bachelor with a clean-butchered dick *and* an empty house. And another thing. Bra E practically lived with Barney. People who know these things say *that's* who started 7678B's famo dances. That it was Bra E's business—the women gyrating like holy ghosts, bare bottoms and lipsticked vulvas riding wild accordion song. And the men— jostling, singing, their voices traveling from Old Potch Road to Orlando and back again; their full throttle tenors growing ever thicker and stiffer.

But some things, like that whole famo business, some things are better left unsaid. Take Barney. We knew what Barney was, even if *he* didn't or tried to deny it. We also knew that's how he got the sickness. From Bra E.

At the time of Bra E's death, Barney was sicker than Freddy Mercury's final act. Some said it was God's punishment for all Barney's wicked debauchery during those crazy famo years. The prophet said it was Barney's ancestors—upset by Barney and his twin sister's sharp split, parting the ancestors' blood. So Barnabas sent word for Ousie Boytjie, who was fetched from some squatter camp to 7678B.

Of course, nobody sensible trusted this prophet. He was just another unemployed, uneducated high school dropout when he woke up with the holy ghost strapped to his tongue one day and professed to amaPenticost. Naturally, the Enlightened Christian Gathering pinned a Star of Bushiri onto his scrawny drawers and claimed him their own. That's all it took for the cheeky youth to start handing out prophecies. He'd wear white raised-rubber shoes and stand on street corners asking the lamb's blood to rain on the faithful.

People mostly humored him, but after he poured Coca-Cola for Barnabas and Barnabas showed strange signs of recovery, the prophet's business boomed. He rented more shack space from his landlady and opened a thriving Coca-Cola *Shop-in-a-Fridge*. His landlady charged extra for electricity, even though she herself pilfered power from Eskom's streetlights. And yet even still, the prophet couldn't stock the Coke fast enough. People reported their children were suddenly cleverer at school, that their thick gathered senyama—those veils of black cloudy bile—that they just drifted off and went missing.

And so it seemed to us that Barnabas and Boytjie were finally on the mend. She moved in and took care of forgotten things. Like painting 7678B a color very much the insides of a woman. Like putting up matching lace curtains and installing an electric stove. Everyone wondered where such good money came from. Didn't she come from the squatters? Hadn't she been left penniless, after a failed and barren marriage?

The rumors swirled, stirring up long spoiling sin. Only now it seems obvious, Ousie Boytjie must've been listening. Must've even scattered some of those rumors herself; they were wild, self-breeding seeds about her bottomless wealth, taking root from ear to eager ear.

And when we were whipped into the fever pitch of a frantic frenzy, when everyone wondered what her business was, Ousie

Boytjie slaughtered a bull to mark her bank's official launch. The People's Power & Millionaires' Club, she called it. The whole of Diepkloof came.

It was a hot day. The sun cast a glare over an enormous white tent, which arrived two days before the bull and was hitched in the road, right in front of 7678B. Phela this was no ordinary basic lowlife tent!

This was a top-class white wedding cake–like building that could fit a whole nation inside, including the moon and the stars. Its walls had make-believe windows—clear plastic with white trimming. Its three spires swept up, proud, standing very tall above all the asbestos roofs and coalstove chimneys of Soweto. We all admired it.

—I thought she'd rent a stretcher? Eddie asked.

—Ha! You don't know Ousie Boytjie, Zuka sneered.

—Only top of the class for Mrs. Madam.

—Ja. But this is just a show-off, man, Professor insisted.

—Why didn't she just rent Nkandla then?

—Hai suka wena, Prof! Tallman replied.

—Don't be jealous. Just because this isn't that refugee crisis you married your daughter under.

—Kakaka kakaka kakaka!

We burst into careless, splattered laughter, like a broken sewer pipe.

—Mxm, Professor sucked his teeth. Then shouted, Laugh all you want!

He paused, baring his teeth, chipped gold cap shining through.

—"Refugee crisis," keee-keee-ki! Professor mocked us, "Refugee crisis," hahaha! *That* daughter of mine has a M-R-S certificate, my dear. And you? What about you, Tallman? Who's fathering your daughter's strays?

Tallman stood up, his head threatening to pierce the tent spire.

—C'mon, Prof! Tallman said. Don't even start. Don't make me
tell it in the people how your fancy new son-in-law is the same
cross-eyed nephew you *yourself* loaned five thousand rands to
pay you *his* lobola. And on installment, nogmal!

We all sucked teeth. Laughed steely. Riling on these two saw-
toothed tongues.

—But serious! Kortman Mike asked. This tent. How much did
Boytjie pay?

—Hey, ja, Professor responded. Me too, I really can't say. Mini-
mum eight thousand rands. We paid half that for my daughter's stretcher. And that's not even counting the chairs, the
tables, the tent walls if you want windows, the tablecloths and
what-what . . . They charge extra for all that, you know?

—Tjo! Kortman spat.

—*Eight thousand rands!?!* That's white man money, mos.

—Mxm, Soviet sucked his teeth. Darkies! There you go with that
disparaging kaffir shit.

—'STrue 'sGod, Soviet, Kortman stabbed back. And I know *you*
don't have eight thousand rands lying around at your mother's! So don't black empower me with your big unemployed
English. Even clever blacks, with their fat tenders and beem-
ers. Even *they* don't have that kind of money. Where's this
Boytjie farming it?

—Ha! someone sniggered.

—From the Department of Fraud Control!

Laughter burst again, drowned by the sound of a hoarse
bucky parking just before the tent. It carried a black bull, riding
its rear.

The bull thrust its body 'round and 'round, heavy hooves cir-
cling the hold. Its raw green smell pressed into the heat. The air
made room without moving, swelling with grassy fetor. We stood
watching from under the tent, still chewing fat.

—C'mon, man. Bucs' voice rose over Shivambu's. How do *you* know that cow's a Brahmin?

—Because I know! Shivambu insisted.

—*Because you know?* Since when do you farm, Shivambu?

—Since your wife started charging in maize!

A clean cloud of cackling burst open. Ousie Boytjie and the bucky driver crowded around the beast at the back of the van.

Its eyes had a lazy sparkle to them, as if God poured black liquid gold into big round disks and carefully glued long lashes onto the hot batter. Its might—its fearsome neck and stout and sturdy legs—was fenced in behind wooden slats that formed the bucky's holding pen. Boytjie locked eyes with the beast and looked very puffed with herself. Her buttocks suddenly seemed fuller, sat higher.

Her Sunlight soap–green overall was ankle length, but all the buttons to just above her knee were undone, so that her dimpled flesh rolled playfully out of the smock whenever she moved from the parked vehicle to onlookers in the nearby tent. There were deep stains on her overall, and her head was covered in a homely scarf. Still, Boytjie was beautiful. She was one of those odd beauties whose stray parts wouldn't make pretty on anyone else. Her elephant ears and kitten nose made no sense at all, but somehow, on Boytjie's face, everything conspired into a meaningful whole. She was smiling that disarming grin that made you forget her toothiness, that convinced you her wide gap wasn't something missing but some elemental filler for the very word: beautiful.

—Lekae bathong? she greeted everyone, shaking hands and playing politician.

—Shame, bathong, she said.

—Thank you for coming.

We all crowded around her expectantly, the tent-gathering growing, as though she were about to perform some small miracle and we'd all eat holy bread. A few of us even stepped to the back of the bucky to help unload the bull. The driver—a tokoloshe-looking man who stood pygmy height and had their stout midget muscles and hairy upstanding ears—slipped a loose noose around the bull's neck. He spoke a separate language with the beast, leading it slowly out of the wagon and reassuring it when it sensed danger. Ousie Boytjie walked ahead, directing the bull and driver into 7678B's yard.

As the bull entered 7678B, the front iron gate shuddered. Tom's Eden was long gone—part of Boytjie's purge. Instead, she'd stripped 7678B to bare earth, then sealed this rich red dirt under sand and cement and turned the green garden into gray gravel.

Bucs and Soviet steadied the gate, Tokoloshe-driver coaxing the bull inside, until it stood against a wall ringing the enclosure. Midget man then used the rope lassoed around the beast's neck to tether it to a steel bar.

After the bucky took off and the bull seemed settled, Boytjie gave a speech. And you know what? Professor was right all along—Boytjie might as well have hired Nkandla, she was so bloody chuffed with herself. *And yet.* The way she stood in the middle of the tent, it was still with befittingly womanish modesty and plain speak. You had to appreciate and give her that.

—Ehhhh! Thank you, honorable members of The People Power and Millionaire Club.

Today is a very important day for The People Power and Millionaire Club.

Ousie Boytjie spoke in English, tripping her tongue and earning her snickers.

—Ja. Me I am forming The People Power and Millionaire Club. Or PPMC as the people call it. In it was the year twenty twenty-two.

—"Me I am amaMillion" . . . dololo, Kortman mimicked Boytjie in whispers.

Professor, at the back of the tent, cupped his hand to his mouth, suppressing a laugh. Soviet and some others held their phones in the air, recording cheap laughs we'd all enjoy later. The bull, now alone in the yard, started fussing. People turned around to look but the animal seemed secure. Ousie Boytjie plunged on.

—Ladies and Gentlemen, she said.

—Girls and Boys. There will be so much money that it is enough. It is already busy going around, this money: In Nigeria. In Kenya. In China—they are all habing it.

—Even the Crocodile in Zimbabwe! Yes! He is habbing it. So why not us in Mzansi? Why we cannot also be habing it?

—People they are getting free from the struggle! Money struggle. Suffer struggle.

—*Mara Howcome? Ousie Boytjie?* people is asking me, *How can we make it must happen now?*

Boytjie raised her pitch here, pantomiming her "people."

—Well, me I am want to tell you the very free and easy truth:

—It is because of The People Power and Millionaire Club!

She gave a dramatic pause here, before her hands fired this way and that, gesticulating like a preacher struck by lightning.

—Because I was living in a squatter not even knowing one plus one before PPMC. Because my brother needed simple medicine and PPMC helped me I buy this one. Because you see me bafowethu, I am living nje ngamaMillionaire.

—Look at my house! Boytjie shouted, pointed at 7678B.

We searched the identical houses diligently, as though Boytjie would indeed produce President Zuma's Nkandla amid the gray railroad-style three room cinderblocks.

—Look at my brother! she exclaimed.

—Barney! she pecked her neck up, searching through the crowd.

—Stand up, Barney! Let the people see you. Let them look for what The People Power and Millionaire Club it done.

Bra Barney stood. Everyone in the tent strained in their white plastic chair or standing position, necks craning, to see Barney. His health stamped out the snickering. If we were skeptical about the source of Boytjie's money, we were cocksure we could trust what the three-lettered curse had made out of Barney's flesh and blood. We'd seen it with our own eyes. Barney had been as good as dead. And only a few short months ago. Ousie Boytjie *had* healed him. Yes, the prophet was involved, but there was money to pay the prophet and money to pay for medicine.

We leaned in closer—ears eager, bellies roaring.

—People Power and Millionaire Club is a investment donation, Boytjie said.

—If you put in ten thousand rands, you going we give you ten thousand rands in thirty days. And then also thirty percent interest we give. So thirteen rands grand total! Before a month it finish!

At this point, the bull grew louder. Ousie Boytjie gave some Sotho instructions midway through her speechifying to fasten that monster tight, joking her ancestors were getting restless for the bull's blood.

—Ja, man. Boytjie continued.

—The suffer is enough. The struggle is finish bafowethu. And you know, in People Power and Millionaire Club, we don't like we eat alone. That's why today I say thank you very much my ancestors and share my good luck with you. You must also share the good news, phela. If you bring two new members to be joining PPMC, your donation coming back with *one hundred percent*! You donate ten thousand rands, we invest back inside your pocket twenty thousand rands, my friends! In thirty days! Show me the bank that can do this one for you?

Someone's hand shot up as if to answer. It looked like Happy, one of Caretaker's great-grandsons. Boytjie smiled stupidly, as if her powers could dip our blackness into ocean water and turn us Black American. The boy Happy tried to raise his voice, but his alarm caught in a stutter. He was slow in the head that one, a real malkop—people didn't pay him much mind. And then Happy started running in the tent, shoving bodies aside, trying to get to 7678B's gate. But it was already too late. Even with the front only narrowly open, the bull made its escape.

—Yoooh Mma-we! Yoooh! Boytjie shouted.

—Thibang bathong! Thibang! she cried, hands on head and buttocks fluttering upward in swift motion.

—Stop that cooooow, man! She was running too now, hiking
up her overalls to thick thighs that showed surprising athletic
grace.

—Thusang bathong! Boytjie screamed.

—Help! Help!

But even Happy couldn't keep up with the bull. Somehow, the bovine had loosened the knot binding its hinds. It was already beyond 7678B's enclosure when Happy first noticed it; it was now halfway up the street, tail wagging Happy and Boytjie into the chase.

The few who hadn't come to Boytjie's party spilled out of their houses and into the street, hands on hips. People were laughing. Wide open-mouth laughter, head thrown back laughter. Lurid laughter so mouthwateringly thick and juicy, sleeping cousins had to be woken from post-midnight shift naps; chore-bound daugh-ters had to be beckoned to come out—*Quick!* Soapy hands still dripping wet with suds.

—Woza! voices called.

—Hei wena, come! Quick!

—Dude, you *have* to see this, the Model C set tweeted.

—It's Ousie Boytjie, Mma! She's catching a cow . . .

Old Man Madala, a fresh cigarette in his mouth, almost fell off his perch screaming for Uncle Albert.

—Hei, man! Boet Albert? Make quick, man! Barnie's sister's out here hunting chow!

The bull charged up the street. It ran how those TV cowboys ride rodeo, galloping on three hooves until it altogether hopped out of the loosened knot cuffing its legs. Ousie Boytjie, out of breath, stopped to shout for help.

—You useless stjupid swines! she hollered.

—Standing there like you're watching a bloody bioscope!

—Make fast, man!

—Get me some rope! Someblerrybody bring me rope!

Eventually, the bull was caught. By none other than the conniving prophet. He was returning from a rare house call in Orlando when he came face to face with the jailbreak beast. Not knowing its surrounding drama, he untied his braided belt to rope the animal and steer it to his shack. Of course, catching it increased his respect enormously. Although there were also some who suspected the whole thing for show, a silly sham between a shotgun prophet and squattercamp banker.

At any rate, we followed behind the prophet, shepherding the captured bull back to the slaughterhouse, 7678B. We were feeling very triumphant and full of spirit. The meat would be doubly tender and the brewing beer well deserved. And so Ousie Boytjie left the mighty speeches behind and got on with the real task of the day, offering the ancestors this bullish sacrifice.

And how the beast cried. Barney's blade could've spliced dry air it was so sharp. It slid through the bull's skin like hot fat greasing an iron skillet. Six men held him still, clinging onto his cloven hooves to pin him down. He lay on his side. The knife struck swiftly but the bull's bellow, at first a low and guttural roar, grew raspy and quick—high-pitched and full of hot and desperate breath; his flailing tail a flag in the wind.

Working his thin long spear, Barney jiggled into the flesh again and again, leaning his shoulders and thighs into the effort, his forearm muscles standing pronounced over veins. The bull kicked. Shook his head no, yes, no. His eyes—those full moons filled with gleaming black gold—softened, then slackened. Cried. When his voice finally collapsed, the weight of his might lay heavy on the cemented ground. Ousie Boytjie washed her hands in his blood before bringing a large, widemouthed basin to the cut, collecting the life milking away in a determined river.

Tjo! Let me tell you we feasted like black bin Ladens that day! Bin Laden *before* Obama Mau-Mau'd that Muslim jihad business. Each one of us devouring what might as well have been seventy-two virgin brides. There was more meat and beer than any stomach could hold. It was only fair for people to lionize Ousie Boytjie, to make up songs about her good cheer and praise the People's Power & Millionaires' Club—bound to bring us all good fortune. The whole affair sounded like a long SABC One commercial praising ourselves, *Simunye-e-e-e!* Bellies full and bladders bleary-eyed, people ignored the bad luck surrounding the runaway's slaughter, and the audible thirst in Boytjie's evangelism.

Soon enough, even the filthiest gossips gave up digging through Boytjie's dirt. A year after PPMC's launch, she drove a pink Land Rover with custom number plates: CATCH UP! Members of PPMC dropped her first name altogether, preferring the honorific and standalone *Ousie*. Everyone in the township knew this Ousie, knew how high off the hog she lived; and everyone seemed to have a story about how her donation and investment club had saved a friend's house from the auction block or rescued a single mother's children from certain hunger. The People's Power & Millionaires' Club was so busy and widespread, its members even shared a special salutation, *"Let Kingdom Come."* True believers called themselves the "Highly Favored" and competed for Boytjie's attention, bringing their Ousie many gifts and plenty small favors. Business was good.

Barnabas should've been happy. And he *was* happy, until he heard what the Professor had to say. And maybe he shouldn't've listened. Because we all knew Professor was green with envy. Because wasn't *he* the one who'd made this street famous? Back in 1975, Comfort Goapele Soga, aka Professor, was the only high school student to pass his matric exams in all of Diepkloof. Wasn't *he* the one who attended university, koTurfloop? So what if he'd dropped out? Who else had even a snotlick of Professor's education? Certainly not a shack-and-banking sham with broken English!

So of course, Professor wanted to shock Barney out of his potbellied lull. Even if it was only a smallanyana slice of time standing between Barney and this bit of news, whether Professor told him or not. Such gossip travels Soweto like hungry cancer cells on the lookout for fresh flesh.

From Dlamini for instance, we'd heard about a cripple jailed for trespassing into his own house. He'd lived there his whole life. His father, the horny old bastard, had married some street madam who charmed him with God knows what. Before the old man could be lowered underfoot, his straatmate wife had turned against her step lot—emptying their house, locking the front gate and serving restraining orders. When the cripple wheeled through the front gate anyway, Street Madam—who we heard was already married to another old and dying man—called in the cops.

In Mphefeni, an old pensioner learned that her brother, the family drunk, had bet their house in a bad game of cards. A knock came just shy of the drunk's burial.

—You have until the end of the funeral, the stranger said, flashing the family's title deed, now in this stranger's very own name, before shifting furniture and making himself comfortable.

We'd even heard about a high-class feud involving a toothless nobody and her billionaire niece. The billionaire sued her nobody aunt over the family's standard-issue, apartheid matchbox three-room. *Imagine that!*

And so, by the time Professor told Bra Barney what he had to say, the twins' second intifada was on. The renewed war broke out in an inescapable announcement:

BLOODY BOYTJIE! 7678B screamed. HOW COULD YOU? CHANGE *MY* TITLE DEED TO *YOUR* NAME? YOU BLOODY SWINE FROD BACKSTAB! SIES!!!

Barney had the whole thing graffitied in a wrap-around spray paint that repeated throughout 7678B's outsides like unfortunate wallpaper. You could read the full manifesto from either side of the street. The words were large block letters that demanded full attention, the same defiant font and furor favored by Comrades' FREE MANDELA wall sprays throughout the struggle. And you could tell they were thrown up at night, under cover of dark. The black paint ran out in certain letters and dripped globs of ink elsewhere, like a reluctant shadow.

The day the graffiti came up with the sun, it was a big spectacle. Everyone gathered, jaws dropping into agape hands; hands held under chin in case the whole mouth should fall from shock. Ousie Boytjie did not come out that day. People could see her pink Land Rover parked in the yard. But no one saw her, not even at the window, parting curtains.

Eventually, we grew bored with the specter and accepted

7678B's defiled face as part of the township's charm, like the new welfare class of teenage mothers or stray dogs rambling through roadside trash. Turn left at the house with the fraud sign, someone might direct a lost driver. You know the one. It's pink with loud shouting swear words? Oh, yeah! the Johnny-come-latelys would beam. We passed a half year like this, the second intifada fading from urgent gossip.

The only person bothered by the whole fracas seemed the same fool fomenting the foofaraw himself. Barney was so busy shitting in Boytjie's watering hole, he seemed to forget he drank from her gourd.

—Boytjie's bank is fake, Barney preached to anyone who made the mistake of greeting him.

—Lekae, Bra Barney? that someone might've asked, how are you?

—A fokkken spaza bank, Barney would reply.

—Fish! Professor laughed, teasing Barney. When did you come out the can?

—Please man, Barney! Soviet would add. Don't let jealous speak for you.

—Or your sickness! Phuza snickered.

And it was true Barney's sickness was returning. It was also true he'd started disappearing for weeks at a time, resurfacing in flashy cars driven by motley men. But for all that strange business and his loathsome Boytjie battles, Barney was in fact the sensitive one. Things lodged different in him. The few Shakespeare lines both twins picked up as young kids, for example, took root in Barnabas like a determined sapling searching for light. He recited what he remembered with the same depth of feeling with which he held on to injury.

On the other hand, Boytjie was like a slick seal: everything slinked off her back.

Of course, the real truth of Barney's sickness was his incurable shame; Barney's shame out-poisoned any virus squatting in his veins. He was rotting, inside-out, like a worm-cored apple—pus-stuffed but still hanging from a tree. His inner anguish a patient and silent killer.

And the bolder his malady distended, the fatter the rest of us grew from Boytjie's bank. Even as Hawks descended on 7678B, we just reasoned they were like the rest of the ANC—Africans baNeedang Corruption—out on the prowl, fishing for palm grease. The People's Power & Millionaires' Club was in the news by then, Ousie Boytjie even appearing on TV. That's how we learned it wasn't exactly her bank. There was a spectacled man in Moscow who phoned in and did most of the talking. Boytjie and the other Highly Favoreds were just in the camera shot for support, to show real members satisfied with the bank.

Afterward, Professor called the Muscovite a fake Communist. He's just like Soviet, Professor said. But watching the TV show, we'd agreed with the serious-looking man who'd asked, Who is suffering from all the profits going to poor people and all the charity work PPMC does? Maybe the media, you're the only lot complaining. Everyone in the community, the Muscovite said, all the People's Power and Millionaires' Club members are very happy. At that point, the camera zoomed to Ousie Boytjie, smiling earth-wide, a *Made in China*–size gap wedged between her front teeth.

Barney disappeared again. When he resurfaced, he stayed with the prophet. He complained about a dark cloud hovering over 7678B: senyama. People started believing. The white man's bank came and took Boytjie's pink Land Rover away. Strangely, Barney didn't comment. Even when we gossiped we'd seen Boyt-jie walking *on foot*! Whoever would've thought they'd ever see a thing like *that*?!?!

Instead, Barney just became sadder than his sickness. He spent most of the day reclined in the sun, on the stoep of the prophet's narrow shack. He didn't even react when we heard and told him that 7678B's title deed was under investigation.

As for Boytjie, it was harder and harder to parcel whether she was sinking or swimming. Everyone seemed to have their own story: That the bank *was* in fact a fraud, Madoffing the poor. That the bank was merely rebooting and real risk appetites would soon be handsomely rewarded.

The only thing we one hundred percent knew from the prophet was that Boytjie was still secretly supporting Barnabas. For some strange reason, she kept the prophet on the books, seeing to Barney's food and now useless medicine. Maybe it was guilt, people said. Or maybe she was still Highly Favored. Charity was, after all, a core tenet of PPMC membership. In any event, the only person beyond speculating was Barney himself. Him and his twin were past counting intifadas—they were living in a full-blown war.

And then the blaze burned. Twice. We only believed him after, but the prophet had in fact forewarned of hellfire.

Boytjie was supervising some longtime members who came to use her electric stove. Her oven was more reliable than their coal kilns and Ousie knew several bake recipes, where most women only knew one. And they were baking that one recipe—township scones.

Agnes later said it was Seipati who stacked all the Rama margarine covers on the stove's burner, idiotically forgetting Rama is wrapped in paper. Malefa's version accused Ntsiki of turning the oven to 450°C when Ousie said 200°C.

—You know Ntsiki likes pretending boklever, Malefa said, tongue tutting.

—Like she can read!

It only took a snap for the fire to flare, flinging Boytjie's stainless-steel appliances into flames, as well as the old linoleum flooring and wooden front door. Naturally, we collected a small donation for Boytjie. The money must've helped a little, but she got a dizzying sum of hard cash from some insurance scheme. That's what started her remodeling 7678B into Monte Casino.

For some reason, Boytjie got it in her head to build up, to add a second floor instead of extending backwards. But 7678B, being a three room matchbox, had its fourth wall conjoined with the neighbors'. The two houses formed a long six room car train, really, split down the middle by a siamese wall yoking two separate households together. Building a second floor meant worrying that fourth wall. And there was no way such a mission wouldn't rankle 7678B's conjoined neighbor, Baba Timoti.

People who know everyone's business say Baba Timoti was born fathering. He seemingly came to Jo'Burg already preaching, already holding his Apostle shepherd staff in one hand and an indecipherable Bible he couldn't read in the other. When he wasn't tending his nomadic flock, Baba Timoti was a security guard who carried a sjambok, even though people claimed they'd seen Baba Timoti with a real gun. Rubbish! Baba was too old for guns. Besides, he was the kind of security whose main deterrent is the shame of robbing an old man.

In addition to night watchman, Baba Timoti ran a very healthy paraffin and peanuts business. The peanuts came with his wife, who traveled frequently to Eshowe. The paraffin was siphoned from Timoti's mantshingilane job. People loved Baba. His paraffin was cheaper than everyone else's, and when the going got really rough, Baba sold on credit.

Of course, this didn't stop anyone from foulmouthing his dirt. He sired half his flock, people said. And even though it was hard believing young girls would splay themselves for fuel, all Timoti's young female congregants grew heavy about nine months into churching with his crowd.

After that first kitchen fire, 7678B looked nothing like itself. The before and after was made all the more real by 7678A—Baba Timoti's original matchbox—shadowing 7678B; a shantytown huddle glued to Sandton Sun. 7678B's graffiti was long gone. But so was the back kitchen door, the single front window, the original three room layout, and even the cement plastered yard. In their place stood a double-storied monster with huge gaping windows that looked down the whole street. A tall wall fortressed the perimeter so we couldn't see inside. To top it all off, Boytjie built a new entrance with an electric, remote controlled gate. It was all very monied and very *Look At Me*. 7678A was beaten down by 7678B's new money top-shayelaness.

And then the fire returned.

This time, Baba was on non-speaking terms with Boytjie. Construction on 7678B had taken months—months of sawdust, loud hammers, and shared wire blackouts. The final straw was the fourth wall. Of course, Boytjie paid to build it back up, but for a few weeks so many bricks were knocked out that Baba stared into Boytjie's dining room whenever he settled in front of his television. Turn your TV around then, Boytjie barked at Baba's complaints.

—That bloody blixem Baba, Boytjie told her Highly Favored.
—With *his* fokken fake priesthood! Telling *me* what to do?

But some of her own Highly Favoreds now relied on Baba's fuel. And they didn't take too kindly to her latest splash of nouveau riche, what with their own fortunes having drowned with the bank's.

People say Baba Timoti did nothing to stop the second fire while he could. That he fueled the fledgling flames with his illicit paraffin and cared only about rescuing his white Apostle robe and shepherd staff. The thing is, Baba Timoti's whole house also burned down. What kind of fool would do that? What we know for one hundred percent is that the whole thing started in liminal dark, in that magical devil hour just before first light.

It was summertime. Even with nothing, people were feeling very festive and looking forward to the holidays. There was even a rumor that Boytjie would host a fresh slaughter braai on Christmas. Like that wild launch party some years back now, the one with her runaway bull.

It sounded like a small chatter when it started. A private conversation. As if 7678B wanted to whisper to itself, or murmur its secrets to 7678A next door. We slept through it. We heard nothing, turning, each in our beds—in wet sheets from a bladder-blubbering child or in the slack arms of a spent, illicit lover.

We woke to its wonder. It sounded like labored breathing, a deep thing stuck in the chest. Baba Timoti's flock was somehow already gathered outside, flinging sand in plastic buckets and hosing water in every direction. The fire hurled its hot phlegm at them, spitting back small specks of thrown earth. As it unfurled, it rolled us all into the street, where we stood shouting against its high cackles and mighty rubble. Ousie Boytjie was still inside.

It was probably too late by the time Baba Timoti raised his voice in a pitch of prayer, but we were so desperate, we raised our voices also, trying to sing over the fire's loud laugh, something that might soothe it or force God into listening. The fire raged. Barnabas, who hardly came out of the prophet's room anymore because of the sickness eating his insides, he floated at the edge of the crowd before slinking from us, into the house. Professor ran after him, but Bra Barney leapt with the force of someone running for his life.

—Boy-Boy! Barney cried.

—Boy-Boy!

It took Soviet and Zuka to muscle Professor down, to stop him from chasing Barnabas into the blaze.

We stood in front of 7678B, watching. The fire clapped its own appreciation, having finally defeated us. No one seemed to remember Baba's song. We stood there, mute, in total submission, watching a full fire fight its own way down.

Some people claim they saw Boytjie dancing in the flames. Others say she was in fact the fire, that her restless spirit combusted, taking everything with it. Hai! It's hard to say.

When the bushblaze had completely burned out and its ashes were now smoldered to dust, we found Boytjie's bones curled like a fetus in motherwomb. People who wanted to believe it say she slept through the fire, that she felt nothing and so should we. Professor and the others looked for signs of Barney in 7678B's remains. Nothing turned up. Barney disappeared without trace, as sudden as the flareup of a fresh intifada.

# Dr. Basters

*I knew a John once. In graduate school. Kampala, Univer-*sity of Buganda. Spindly man. Thick rimmed spectacles and a correspondingly milky take on a world that tolerated his foolishness. Bible thumper. The continent had already smoldered into some foreigner's amebic fantasy of it, and all Johnnie could see was every preacher they sent in to mop up their shame.

—Trevor Huddleston?

His voice always got squeaky around his shaky arguments, *What about the right and honorable Father Huddleston?*

I heard he became a preacher, John David. The right and honorable Father John David Mutanda. Died of whoring. The earliest onset of AIDS in our circle. It was worse than witchcraft back then. A conspiracy better than anything all the CIA spooks and jives could plant in a windowless room.

Finally—the witchtalk concluded—finally something strong enough, something smart enough to rein in our enviable manhood. And sure, it *could've* worked, I suppose. But these CIA sorts have always underestimated us. I mean, it didn't stop *me* from fucking around.

And let's not pretend we're just big-dicked tribal ignorami whose only understanding of disease is sorcery. Canker culling-weapons have a long and storied history with this lot—ask Kwame

Ture about catching stray cancers. And if anybody thought Tus-
kegee was their worst, understand we're talking about the same
Neros who actually *paid* syphilis-ridden whores in Guatemala to
sleep with imprisoned subjects. A fucking *study*, they called it!
Paid the harlots fat and honest hardworking tax greenbacks.

Qué imposible, you say? Fact-check me then. Shit's in the
motherfucking *New York Times*! So please. Understand: *that's* the
level of devilment we're dealing with.

And yet. *I'm* the crazy pan-Africanist at department kowtow
pow-wows when I point out the obvious danger letting them
study even one patient in the name of Ebola.

—But Professor, some little Johnnie invariably squeaks.

—Professor Basters! Ebola is bleeding West Africa dry. Just today
I heard them say ten thousand dead in Sierra Leone.

Ten! Thousand! *Lives!* he'll repeat, as if I've forgotten how to
count. Yes, I'll shake my head, acquiescing to what he sees: a
porky old man who's taken to corsets and garters to gird a soft,
depressing udder; a blind haruspex and complete stranger lost in
his homeland.

And anyway, what's the use of trying to school the Johnnies of
this world? Why should what I say equal two bobs farting around
his mushy mind?

I mean, if a real man like New Orleans' André Cailloux could
die while facing down a Confederate artillery shell, and yet *still*
have his body rot in the ground for forty-seven days because his
Union general refused to acknowledge black valor, what will *not*
be forgotten? Nothing, dear little Johnnie. Nothing endures.
Everything, forgotten.

I read somewhere that Siksika First Nation Chief Crow-
foot wanted to know the same exact thing. *What the fuck's the
fucking point?* Except my man let out the kind of big-bang bib-
lical verse you could only belt out if your daddy's name was

Istowun-eh'pata—Packs A Knife—and your favorite wife, from a swarm of ten, no less, was a badass bitch called Cutting Woman. —"What is life?" Chief asked.

"It's the flash of firefly in the night.

It's the breath of buffalo in wintertime.

It's the little shadow that runs across the grass and loses itself in the sunset."

*That's* what the Chiefman said. Talk about a grand fucking finale and middle finger to death!

Krish used to smile when I'd ask her, What's the point? Who knows? she'd shrug. But she knew. Her eyes knew. Witch eyes, Krish's. Tachyons that could fission eternity into concrete atoms of dirt. Could make dust of anything dense and invincible, mold the ethereal into something tangible.

We'd be lying on sweated backs, Krish smoking, me panting. The bed balanced on metal frames. It was an old hospital bed, diamond wire-mesh supporting loud springs. Not much else in that arsebare room. A busted black-and-white television someone abandoned. Rusty hangers we retrograded into rabbit ears quoting the screen. And curtains Krish put up. Looked like sorry sacks of moldy sari, if you asked me. I mean who wants samosa-smack sifting through their loveshack? But Krishna insisted on fully dressing the windows. And really, I'm a reasonable man—can't let prejudice get in the way of Grade A pussy.

Because Krish was a beast. I mean, talk about Kama Sutra! That woman could've schooled Vātsyāyana on a thing or two. Her shaftman flytrap was pudenda genitale par excellence.

She had enormous talent, Krish. Could've been anything she wanted. *Anything.* But she caved. And who could blame her? Solitary will fuck the sanity out of your smugness. Those bastards came for her when they couldn't find me. Bait. I should've seen it coming. Should've left *with* her. If my eyes weren't so tightly

shut between that puddinged pussy, I could've rewritten the
end, drafted something less predictable. But shit happens: Love.
Regret. Do I regret losing Krish? And what my disappearance
cost her?

Blur and numbness, those years raising fists. Weekends marching, *Amandla!* Blowing up power plants, burning Boere crops.
Fear was a constant, a giant unspoken cantankerous cyst. And
then this Indian girl—caught right inside that cyst, where everything was sore. Everything forgotten: dreams, self, right, wrong.
What the fuck were we fighting for? Everything, forgotten. All
our emergency exits fleeing the cyst—resistance, exile, double dealing, hiding or disappearing underground—everything
turned into maiming ourselves or opening ourselves to ambush.

Indian girl who could've been anything. Krish! Our babies
would've been beautiful.

She sent me a parcel before she died. All my little gifts. Carefully sorted, packaged, mended even. That should've clued me
to her end. Ordered. Planned. Fully and soberly considered. But
instead of reading her clues when the package arrived, I carried
us back inside that flat, tried to imagine the room sweating its
samosa smell, Krish drawing her tatty curtains when I returned
from trips we both pretended never happened. Tried to lean my
body into each envelope, will their deep-fried stench deep inside
my lungs.

Ahhh, Krish! Look at me. Daydreaming of curried pussy like
these lovesick Yankees—I've got hundreds of dead soldiers spoiling on my desk. Nothing but Pleasant Unthank named, Gettys-
burg battle crowned, Yoknapatwapha County–bound southerners
and lovesore Yankees. They warred through their Great Rebellion, weepy love letters in hand. No wonder it took them four
years to vanquish the South.

And now they sit at my desk, still slugging it out:

—Slavery?

—Bad!

—Confederacy?

—Ehhhh . . . Maybe not so bad?

Reams of them on the page, fighting for space alongside my long crumpled thoughts, expired subscriptions and stale cigar butts.

Suffocating.

I need some fokken air. Krish and these Yankees? They're all gone.

Me?

I bloody well need some air.

A rg! Blerry bastard. I'm gatvol with this filthy m'gokgo. Wrote to the muni twice already, tried to warn some sense into them: If I catch that stray piece of shit on my property again, SPCA will have more meat to pack off than all the slaughterhouses on Smoothfield's Cock Lane. But of course, nobody listens to me.

Dear Dr. Basters, they write back. Dr. Ishmael Basters. We received your letter . . . Blah. Blah. Blah. We note your complaint against Mr. Brand of 36 Forbes Road, Blah. Blah. Blah. We informed Mr. Brand—Blah. Blah. Blah. Please also be advised we cannot take your threat of violence to Mr. Brand's dog lightly. Blah. Blah. Blah. . . . Authorities alerted.

Authorities! What authorities? We sitting under a president slowly outshining Mugabe—le Révolutionnaire par excellence— and people still believe in *The Authorities*? What I really should do is stab that guttersnipe right into those rosebushes. You wanna come over here and piss in *my* plants? You wanna leave mountains of your flea-ridden dogshit right here, at *my* gate, right where my own dog knows not to shit? I'll give you something to piss about!

But.

Being the old tannie I've become, I merely shoo the crippled thing away, throw stones and watch it stagger through the same gap in the fence where it entered. I thought about rat poisoning a long time ago. But Kometka has a drunken delusion with the stray. They fondle each other in the nipples like jackrabbits. Kometka even used to share her food with it, until I caught them and put an end to that poppycock. *Lady and the Tramp* my foot. Kometka's vet fees are already breaking my neck. Who knows what wastrel litter we'd end up with if I wasn't vigilant?

I press the remote and wait for the gate. Kometka is close behind, tailing my heels. Wagging and chasing her arse.

Trymore still hasn't trimmed the bougainvillea, it's now climbing over the gate. Asked him last week and again yesterday. It's now mangling the electric fence. You think he'd try these amnesiac monkey tricks on that Boer Brand or on a Mr. Smith? Never. That's just how our people are. You have to carry a big stick and know how to use it. Three hundred and sixty-three years of conditioning bends a man's mind. Mutates him into a monkey mirage mistaken for the man. You're left without choice.

But Trymore? I expected more from Trymore, he's a Zimbo for chrissake. They're hungry, those people. No one jumps over crocodile jaws and into flooded rivers he cannot swim; no one, after all that, crawls under barbed wire snake pits just so he can reach the other side and sit on his arse, arms folded. And yet. I'll have to say it to him again with a bit more bass.

I walk on, dragging the limp left leg along, clearing my mind.

Ahhh, Johannesburg! A growing crime scene against humanity. Just look at this! An entire city begging for demolition. Or at least some sort of fugly intervention. I mean? Any fool who can splash cheap paint on a terra-cotta Lego block and call it something vapid and soft sounding like *Sundown Meadows* gets to be a developer? *How?* And people *pay* for this shit! Look at them. Flashing around in their young-money cars. Flashing and fluttering so feverishly, so violently. Like foul fish on the fry. Just look at them. At how blind they are. Can't even smell their own salt fattening the fires beneath them.

I raise my hand to the poor bastard peddling Coca-Colas to these namby-pambys. He waves. Gestures to a sweating bottle. No thanks, I shake my head. And wait, merciful, in a little shade for the robot to turn green.

While we wait, engines humming and Coke man shouting, dancers turn the zebra crossing into a stage. Their show is a flash flood, white gloves thumping crates and legs Michael Jacksoning hot feverish steps. Quick. Like migrating hooves marking their plain. It's all over before the cars shift gears.

They're new, the dancers. Usually there's a chap dealing out Zulu words. Car-to-car he goes with a sign that says, TRAFFIC LIGHT TEACHER: ZULU WORDS RI + FREE PRONUNCIATIONS. EG, LEARN =FUNDA. He's becoming a big man, our Zulu teacher. Saw him on the six-o'clock news. Can't be better money than the penis "enlargener" who promises to bring back old love. You see a hell o' a lot of open windows when that hustler's out.

Show over, I hobble on.

In the papers today: "PRIME EVIL" IS OUT. Released on good behavior. Put in 19 tax-free years on a 212-year sentence, not counting the two Lifes tagged on for crimes against humanity. Two Lifes is 129.4 years in this country. Add that to the original 212-year sentence and you have 341 years, 4 months. That's 19 down, 322.4 in the balance. Slap on 60 bonus years for his whiteness. Because black lives matter nowhere—we don't fool ourselves in this country. And you've got 382.4 years outstanding. But maybe, these days, things equal out behind bars. Maybe *Pass the soap* still means *Bend over and take this fokken soap*, no matter what your skin buys you outside. So 322.4 years owed. Fair and square.

That's twelve generations. Prime Evil's forebears were just mooring their boats round the Cape 322 years ago, 1693. His then great-granddaddy, let's say a short man with a taste for adventure, was maybe molding bricks to root Kasteel de Goede Hoop—his people's still-standing fortress against kaffirs and sea monsters.

Meanwhile, this granddaddy's eventual "wife"—a shy girl stolen from Dahomey—was busy sprouting tits 322 years ago. Maybe she massaged their rising sting with one hand, leavening her Baas-cum-rapist-husband's bread loaves with the other. Her slave spawn is free today. A vrij burger, as Dutch settlers would've said, a free citizen.

He's probably licking an ice-cream cone somewhere, Eugene Alexander de Kock. Out. Walking, petting his dog. Whites love their dogs. Part of the family, as they say. Chocolate chip mint, I bet. A man as fastidious getting dirty work done as de Kock was stripping, strangling, sjambokking, wetbagging, striking, stroking, smacking, fingering, finishing, basting, burning and braaing black bodies—that man is definitely a man who enjoys chocolate chip mint ice cream. On a cone. Bright green cream bleeding softly, the way mucus slinks down. His hands fisting the pasty wafer cone. Chocolate flecks melting in his mouth. A cool numbness coating each lick. And his pink tongue: in and out.

Out, where everyone can see it.

WHERE'S DE KOCK NOW? headlines shout. As if this lone man—alone in a sea of millions—singlehandedly colonized and raped a land and its people. As if he was the Sunday morning preacher who fenced in his faith and flock, and was also the schoolteacher and his housewife—who tuts her silver tongue only today to feign disgust for the fat that still lines her stomach, doing nothing about the things that cannot, but must be, undone.

Because they—ordinary people that they were; good, common, do-your-duty line of volk—they did not know. How could they know? De Kock busy doing their bidding all on his own? Busy following blind orders from generals and politicians and commanders who also did not know. "PRIME EVIL" WALKS. It's plastered everywhere: on robots, around empty dustbins, below telephone lines, and under load-shedding streetlights.

Inside the parking lot, I remember I needed something. Didn't I? I'll be annoyed if I remember only once I'm home again, reaching for it and then—only then—remembering: Doom! I went out to buy Doom. I would forget, idling as I am. Ambling through Sanlam Centre. Why do they call this place a center? There's nothing central here. Just concrete. A nameless mass of Soviet density. Built by the same people who brought you rooi gevaar. The same fokken generals who "didn't know."

And here's the thing. Here's what those rooi gevaar architects, red danger generals, failed to account for in selling their Cold War malarkey to their foot soldiers—just how sensitive a soldier like Eugene Alexander de Kock could turn out to be.

Because he *is* sensitive. In his way. Fucked up a subordinate once for bedding another's wife. Not the kind of man who'd write *nostalgia* on a Yankee's death certificate. Would've thought long and hard how "Cause of Death: Nostalgia" would've made a soldier's family feel. If the Yankee had an unknown wife or son, for example, how that would've sat with the soldier's son.

Kids are loud in Sanlam Centre. Still in school uniform. All around are black shiny oxfords, knee-high socks, and matching ties in dull grays and forest greens. And blazer crests with leaping springbok and grazing impalas pondering pithy nonsense: Forti

Nihil Difficilius. Yes, indeed. Nothing seems particularly difficult for this lot. Except the small thing of shutting up. Justorum
Semita Lux Splendens. De Kock could've sewn that one on himself, The path of the just is a shining light.

The girls are loudest. Giggling. Their voices throw something
fragile against mall walls, where they stand nursing a standard
performance. Pie City is behind them, a porky man beckoning in
the blue and white logo. The smell is also loud. Like a shock of
stale butter raining indoors.

Hairy men in blooming mustaches and not-grayed-yet trims
ogle the girls. Some even say it outright, Those thighs, sweetie!
Please, my girl, ke kopa those thighs. Just a smallanyana slice
between my pie. Strangers laugh and a round auntie-looking
woman stops—full stop—to stare. I steal my own look the way a
hoary bull spots a kill but dares not charge. Their thighs roll over
each other smoothly, like creamy peanut butter spread over thick
brown bread.

I look away; Eugene would not approve. He is the kind of man
who would spit at such decay, at the bad apples spoiling Pie City.
If he found himself like me—facing Pie City, pretending to sort
a riddle in my wallet, growing something limp but determined
at the sight of the schoolgirls' thighs—he is the kind of man
who'd do something definitive about his perversion. Something
that would've made even Civil War veteran and autopeotomist
W. C. Minor proud.

I decide against entering the mall, wandering its gaping halls.
The courtyard surrounding Sanlam Centre is paved an unimag-
inative color, continuing the rooi gevaar Soviet theme. Three
people fall into line 2.5 meters from the ATM. A small child's
cry echoes.

The courtyard got an *Architectural Digest* roof not so long ago—
part of Randburg's effort to spiff things up. But it only amplifies

the baby's dolphin cries. I look around. My legs are tired. No benches. Instead, low face-brick squares deep enough to double as jacaranda planters litter the courtyard. The trees sway, whistling. They are older than Sanlam Centre. Randburg, possibly. I sit on the edge of a planter.

At the foot of the jacarandas, inside the brick squares, are dense dark vines. The vines are close-cropped and meticulously maintained, like a shaved mountain of pubic hair laid flat into rolling green. I stick my fingers in there, feel about for roots, but the roots are buried deep. All I feel is the silk of the leaves, the furrow of their undersides.

—"He lived there in the unsayable lights

He saw the fuchsia in drizzling noon,

The elderflower at dusk like a risen moon

And green fields graying on the windswept heights."

She isn't addressing me. She isn't even facing me; I only see one side of her whispering mouth and one eye, looking far ahead, to someplace else.

—Semen-us. Hi-moon-us, I beam.

She turns around, laughing.

—*Seamen-ous Hymen-ous?* she repeats.

—And why not? I snigger.

—Well . . . she says, still laughing, unsayable light bouncing off her blackness; a whole and beautiful blackness, capable of swallowing all things.

—You're from Ghana, aren't you? I'm not asking a question.

—Yes. She twinkles.

—How do you—?

—I've been, I say.

So what if I've never traveled north of BOSS cross-border raids?

—Many times, I add.

—What brings you here?

—Oh . . . ehm . . . work, she responds.

Then looks into the distance again. To the someone else "Glanmore Sonnets" was spoken for. She looks nothing like her, but *this* is the Krishna I want to remember. Coal black and purple lips. Quick, bewitching eyes. Krish, my Sidi of Sachin swan! How dare you ever leave me?

A long pause catches. It moves easily between us, like the sound of river water moving quietly, unchased.

—And what about you? she asks. Are you from here?

—My sister! I protest, I sound like a foreigner to you, ehn?

—No. A small laugh.

—That's not what I meant. What I mean is . . . ehm . . . you don't look—

—Japanese?

—No! Loud laugh.

—Chinese?

—Oh, c'mon-oh! You are teasing me.

—No, my sister. I am not. Chinese are officially Black in this country. Ehn-eh!?! Where have you been? Don't you read the papers?

—Please! Mister! She throws back her head, laughing.

—Leave the China alone. You know what I mean.

—I am African, my sister. Despite this fair skin. We arrived on a boat.

—A boat?

—Yes. A rowboat.

We both chuckle. She does not have Krishna's humor, amused only with the macabre.

Sharpeville flattened grown men, but not my Krish. She always found something small but alarming, something frightening to laugh about. Dead again jokes. Mortuary jokes. Bodies piled up jokes.

But tell me, she said, as we tallied state bullets buried in pro-testers' backs, How far did Mr. Dandy expect to run, dressed like Narcissus checking out his tail? It offended me at first. But Krishna had her way. She made the cyst smaller, just laughing at it, made it stand there, naked. Squirming.

—My oupa's oupagrootjie told him we came on a boat. From Angola, I think. Although some say Ceylon.

We were lying on our bellies. Krish smoking. Me, yakking, not listening to her surprise.

—So . . . your people were slaves? She made those perfect halos blowing smoke. Wobbly fog rings wandered from the round of her mouth to the sari curtains in the wind.

—There you go, my Sidi swan. Something else we have in common.

—What do you mean, "in common?" Krishna asked.

—My family came here for work.

—You mean they came on a boat.

—So?

—*So?* So we're the same, Krish. That's what. Your people are nothing. You weren't even touchable where you come from. And you were packed off like dogs, that's what. Slaves. You've probably got even more kaffir in you than me.

I held up my bare arm, comparing it to Krish's navy-dark skin.

—For all I know, *my* family is Indian.

I hadn't meant to, but there was a pressure underneath my words. Krish finished her smoke, the halos now broken. She was pained, I know that now. Old pain. As worn and tasteless as her sari curtains; silk fraying, thread unraveling with the wind.

—What kind of rowboat was this exactly? Ghanagirl asks.

—Oh. It was a wee bit little thing, me lass.

—Oh? she says. I've got her giggling now.

—And who rowed you, mister? Semen-ous Hymen-ous?

—Close, I say.

Then, straight as fact:

—God rowed.

—Ha! Ghanagirl beams.

—I know that's right! She slaps her thigh.

Slim thighs. Clothed thighs. I will my mind to unswerve from the forestfir between their perfect blackness.

—But serious, she says. I already told you I'm from Ghana. Where are you from?

—Kaapstad, I say.

—My people came on a boat. Long time ago. Seamen. From Cape Verde.

—Ah! She lights up. Falar a língua de idade?

—My sister? O! Please-O! Haven't we been chained enough by the white man's tongue? I say, mimicking her accent.

—Why would I take up another one?

—To visit Cape Verde, that's why. And Brazil. Ahhh—I get such saudade for Brazil.

—Sehnsucht? Be careful with that, my dear. Deadly. It's been known to kill.

—Zen-suh-cht? What's that? Is that Afrikaans? she asks.

—German. It's saudade. Black bile. Same thing. A consuming nostalgia for the lost. You can die from that, you know.

I look at her, this blue-black woman with a smile I'd like to stretch into coming winter. She is looking away again, but must feel my eyes burning the light on her skin.

—Saudade took many of my people. We were fishermen. Whalers, to be exact. Harpooners. Coopers. Blacksmiths. Cooks. You name it, we did it. Even a few captains in my blood.

—In Cape Town? She's incredulous.

—Whaling? Oh, I didn't realize . . . In the Cape?

—My sister, I nearly shout. Don't you know you can't trust what these people say about us? Of course we were whaling! We invented whaling!

—Oh, she says.

A second pause. This time, the water rushes. She clears her throat. Her body moves almost imperceptibly, seemingly outside her command, away from mine. A shadow suddenly approaches and just as suddenly engulfs her. The courtyard becomes busy again. Has been busy. Children screaming, mothers fussing, schoolgirls goading leering fathers. Somewhere among them Eugene de Kock is a free man. 'n Vry burger. Watching.

—I was starting to worry, Ghanagirl addresses the shadow.

—Did I leave you too long?

—No, she says, not at all. I was just speaking with our grandfather here. Mister . . . ?

I look at her, for the first time unabashedly studying her. There's a mole under her nose. A blue-black woman with a chain of perfect pearls stuffed in her mouth and a mole under her nose, blacker than sin. Her eyelashes have the luster of velvet moss in lush grasses along a delta. I'd give anything to slide into that greedily growing grass.

I smile, seeing myself through their eyes—a toothless threat. The shadow pulls her into its cast. It looks at me with that look I've come to understand. The department's *He was once a brilliant freedom fighter* look. Brand's *You couldn't do shit if you wanted to* look. The shadow holds out its hand.

—Jappie Basters, I introduced myself, hand outstretched. Twitching.

This was decades ago, before I created Ishmael with his doctorate and world travels. I was still just Jappie then, honest son of a slave. Colored boy fresh uit die Kaap. She gave a soft laugh, my Krish, feebly shaking my hand, but not a mean laugh. Just dancing on the edge of something. Something real, I thought back then. Something sad, I now know.

—Dr. Basters, I say to Ghanagirl.

—Dr. Professor Basters.

—Oh, she says, a weak smile scratching her skin.

—This is Kofi. I'm Julie.

I shake the shadow's hand, remaining seated, and watch them walk off. I don't want to look at their receding long necks, their straight spines and weightless backs. But my eyes follow them anyway. And I know how this sounds coming from "our grand-father" but it happened just the same. Right where the sun splits a man from his shadow, Kofi's shadow turns around and glares at me. His actual shadow—still following Kofi who's now holding the girl—it turns around and stares me down.

There was a funeral I went to recently. One of my supposed friends' family patriarchs. The kind of friend who still needs to believe me a freedom fighter, who'd trade me in—no ques-tions asked—if the PhD were ever found out, or the gallantry unmasked.

The family patriarch lived past one hundred. Or so my friend said. Married my friend's grandmother's sister and produced two daughters, one a cripple and one a dyke, as well as a long-estranged askari son, all wholesome drunks.

Anyway, we're at this funeral and my friend is taking me around, pointing out the chief mourners—the patriarch's daugh-ters, who both look like battered bulldogs, the cousin who makes a living pocketing funeral collections like this one, and other nefarious characters who make up the clan.

—This one packed off with my money, my friend says under his
    breath, fifty rands!

—That one never finished Standard One, even—imagine—
    flunked out of Dom One! And now he's running our ward.

—Ehn!? My friend grins at Dom One.

—Mr. Councilman! my friend says, every tooth prostrating.